"Do You Want To Make Love To Me?"

Macy had asked the question as casually as she would the time. "Well, n-no," Rory stammered.

"Why not?"

He dragged a hand over the back of his neck, suddenly uncomfortable. "I don't know. Probably because you're not my type."

"And what's your type?"

"I like my women soft and feminine."

She glanced his way. "And I'm not?"

"It's not that you're unattractive, it's just that…well, I like women with a little more—" he cupped his hands on his chest to demonstrate "—up front."

She turned to face him. "So you're saying that you wouldn't make love to me because I have small breasts?"

"Well, yeah."

She took a step toward him.

Checking a laugh, he pushed out a hand. "Hey, now. What do you thinking you're doing?"

Her gaze on his, she placed her hands on his shoulders. "Proving a point."

Dear Reader,

We're so glad you've chosen Silhouette Desire because we have a *lot* of wonderful—and sexy!—stories for you. The month starts to heat up with *The Boss Man's Fortune* by Kathryn Jensen. This fabulous boss/secretary novel is part of our ongoing continuity, DYNASTIES: THE DANFORTHS, and also reintroduces characters from another well-known family: The Fortunes. Things continue to simmer with Peggy Moreland's *The Last Good Man in Texas,* a fabulous continuation of her series THE TANNERS OF TEXAS.

More steamy stuff is heading your way with *Shut Up And Kiss Me* by Sara Orwig, as she starts off a new series, STALLION PASS: TEXAS KNIGHTS. (Watch for the series to continue next month in Silhouette Intimate Moments.) The always-compelling Laura Wright is back with a hot-blooded Native American hero in *Redwolf's Woman. Storm of Seduction* by Cindy Gerard will surely fire up your hormones with an alpha male hero out of your wildest fantasies. And Margaret Allison makes her Silhouette Desire debut with *At Any Price,* a book about sweet revenge that is almost too hot to handle!

And, as summer approaches, we'll have more scorching love stories for you—guaranteed to satisfy your every Silhouette Desire!

Happy reading,

Melissa Jeglinski

Melissa Jeglinski
Senior Editor, Silhouette Desire

Please address questions and book requests to:
Silhouette Reader Service
U.S.: 3010 Walden Ave., P.O. Box 1325, Buffalo, NY 14269
Canadian: P.O. Box 609, Fort Erie, Ont. L2A 5X3

THE LAST GOOD MAN IN TEXAS

PEGGY MORELAND

Published by Silhouette Books

America's Publisher of Contemporary Romance

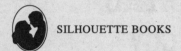 SILHOUETTE BOOKS

ISBN 0-373-76580-0

THE LAST GOOD MAN IN TEXAS

Copyright © 2004 by Peggy Bozeman Morse

This edition published by arrangement with Harlequin Books S.A.

Visit Silhouette Books at www.eHarlequin.com

Printed in U.S.A.

PEGGY MORELAND

Winner of the National Readers' Choice Award and a two-time finalist for the prestigious RITA® Award, Peggy has frequently appeared on the *USA TODAY* and Waldenbooks bestseller lists. When not writing, Peggy can usually be found outside, tending the cattle, goats and other critters on the ranch she shares with her husband. You may write to Peggy at P.O. Box 1099, Florence, TX 76527-1099, or e-mail her at peggy@peggymoreland.com.

To the newlyweds Cara and Cory.
Thank you for choosing the Full Circle Ranch as the
setting for your wedding and for helping us turn it into
a bride's fantasy. May your life together exceed
all your dreams and fulfill all your expectations.

One

The northwest corner of the square at Tanner's Crossing was a beehive of activity. Trucks of every description, mostly of the construction variety, lined the street and ate up what little parking space was left on the adjacent lot that wasn't already barricaded off with signs that read Fresh Oil—Stay Off. Workmen, busy at their individual jobs, sweated beneath a hot midday sun.

Rory Tanner stood in front of the almost-completed building, his thumbs pushed together in front of his face, studying the view through the frame he'd created with his hands.

"I want it to look like a corral," he said, describing the window display as he envisioned it. "Fence posts and some rails. Just a corner, you understand. Not the whole shootin' match. A couple of cactus scattered here and there. Maybe a cow skull propped up in the background. I don't want any mannequins.''

He dropped his hands to shudder. ''Those things give me the creeps. Look like a bunch of stiffs, standing around.'' He waved a hand, indicating the window. ''Hang whatever clothing you want to display from the ceiling. Use fishing line or some such. You can even tack some clothes on the wall, if need be. And boots. Lots of boots. Put 'em on hay bales, a rock, on the floor of the corral we're creating. And use real dirt in the corral. We're goin' for realism here. Lots of color and drama. I want this display to grab a person by the neck and drag 'im into the store.''

He glanced over at the woman who was jotting down notes on a legal pad. ''You get my drift?''

''Yes, I believe I do.'' She lowered the pad to frown at him. ''Though how you think I can pull this off on such short notice is beyond me.''

Grinning, he slung an arm around her shoulders and hugged her against his side. ''Because you're the best window dresser in the state, that's how. Being as this store's in my hometown, it's got to be the best one in my chain. I don't want anybody saying that Rory Tanner does anything halfway. Gotta uphold the family name, you know.''

His mind already jumping ahead to the next problem he needed to deal with, he gave her another quick hug, then strode away.

''Hey, Jim,'' he called to a carpenter perched on a tall ladder propped against the store's front facade. ''Make sure that sign is level. Don't want folks gettin' cricks in their necks trying to read it.''

Chuckling, Jim lifted a hand in acknowledgment and went back to screwing in the bolts that would hold the sign proclaiming Tanner's Cowboy Outfitters.

"Need some help there, Don?" Rory asked a man welding pipe fittings together.

Don flipped up his welding helmet, his shoulders sagging wearily. "I could sure use another set of hands. Gus didn't show today. Probably laid up drunk somewhere. There's another welding helmet on the floorboard of my truck. If you don't mind, grab another couple of pieces of that six-foot pipe from the bed while you're at it."

As handy with a welding torch as he was with a lariat, Rory donned the helmet, flipped back the visor, then pulled several six-foot lengths of pipe from the bed and headed back, toting them on his shoulder. While sizing up the three-foot-high iron railing Don was creating to separate the sidewalk from the parallel parking spaces at the curb, he dragged a pair of leather gloves from his back pocket and tugged them onto his hands, then set to work.

The two men quickly developed a rhythm and, working together, put up two more sections of pipe fencing, before Don pushed back his visor and signaled Rory that he needed to switch out the tanks on his welding machine.

His shirt soaked with sweat, Rory peeled off his helmet. He dragged an arm across his forehead, mopping off his brow as he looked around. Pride swelled his chest. Of all the stores in his chain, this was going to be the flagship, the jewel in a crown of successful retail stores. Rightfully so, since this was his hometown. A lot of folks had wondered if and when he'd put a store in Tanner's Crossing. Until recently, it was the last location he would've considered for expansion.

But since the old man's death, the Tanner brothers were slowly drifting back home, becoming a family again. Ace had come first, when, as the oldest of the brothers, he'd taken over the duties of executor of the old man's estate. He'd set up base at the Bar-T, the family ranch, and taken responsibility for the baby the old man had left behind—literally a doorstep delivery that had left all the brothers standing slack-jawed, wondering what the hell to do with the kid. Then Ace had married Maggie and they'd adopted the baby, which had relieved everyone, Rory included.

Ry was the last to return home, had married and was now busy performing surgeries at the local hospital. Of course, a lot had transpired between Ry's return and him deciding to take up surgery again. But Ry was happy now, happier than Rory remembered him being in years. Most of that Rory attributed to Kayla, Ry's new bride.

In between Ace and Ry's returns, Woodrow had taken himself a wife, a pediatrician who couldn't be any more perfect for Woodrow if she'd been cut and molded just to suit him. Which left Whit and Rory as the only Tanner brothers with their bachelor status still intact. Rory didn't know about Whit, but he intended to hang on to his a sight longer. Maybe forever. He liked women too much to settle down with just one. He liked the softness of a woman, the gentleness, the femininity.

And if the woman stepping out of the Jeep Cherokee that had just driven onto the lot had an ounce of femininity in her, she was hiding it well.

Denim overalls—menswear, in Rory's estimation—camouflaged whatever figure she might have. And that hair! It looked as if she'd lined up with sheep for a shearing and hadn't realized her mistake until halfway through the process. The result was chopped-off shanks of sun-streaked blond hair that hit her about chin length and overlong bangs that she shoved back with an impatient gesture, as she looked up at the sign Jim had finished hanging. A pair of aviator sunglasses hid her eyes, but what part of her face the glasses didn't conceal offered some hope. High cheekbones. A slim nose that on another woman might be considered pixielike. And full, moist lips stained a soft, succulent peach.

It was on those lips that Rory focused as he strode her way, prepared to play host.

"Howdy," he called, and shot her a welcoming smile when she glanced his way. "We're not open for business yet, but if you'd like a personal tour of the store, I'd be happy to oblige."

She gave him a long look from behind her sunglasses, then turned away.

"No, thanks. I saw the sign and hoped I'd find a Tanner here."

Something in her tone told Rory this wasn't a social call, which put him on guard. "There are several Tanners in Tanner's Crossing. Which one are you looking for?"

"Buck." She glanced his way, a brow lifted in question above the rim of her sunglasses. "Do you know him?"

Dread churned in his stomach upon hearing his father's name, but he managed to keep his expression impassive. "Yes, ma'am. It just so happens I do."

She looked around, as if expecting to find Buck. "Is he here?"

"No, ma'am." He eyed her suspiciously. "What would you be wanting to see Buck about?"

She pulled her glasses down her nose and burned him with a look. "That's none of your business."

He bit down on his anger. "Well, I hate to be the one to tell you this, but ol' Buck is dead."

The blood slowly drained from her face. "Dead? But…when?"

"Last fall. Heart attack." He snapped his fingers. "Went like that."

"He can't be dead. I—" She clamped her lips together and looked away.

Rory would swear he saw the gleam of tears in her eyes before she shoved her sunglasses back in place, hiding them. Unsure what to say or if he should say anything at all, he remained silent.

"Family," she said, as if thinking aloud, then turned to him. "You said there were other Tanners in town. Are they related to Buck?"

"Yes, ma'am. That they are. He left behind four sons, a stepson and an infant daughter he never laid eyes on."

"I need to talk to them. Where would I find them?"

"At the Bar-T. The family ranch. It's about ten miles outside of town."

"Can you give me directions?"

"I could," he said, then shook his head. "But it

wouldn't do you much good. The entire place is fenced, with gated security. It'd be easier to gain entrance to Fort Knox than the Bar-T.''

Those moist lips he'd admired thinned to a determined line.

''Well, there has to be a way to get in contact with them. They do have phones, don't they?''

''Unlisted numbers.'' He waited a beat, then added, ''But if you're hell-bent on talking to them, I suppose I could try to arrange a meeting for you.''

''How long would that take?''

He scratched his chin. ''Hard to say. There's a passel of 'em. It'll require some fancy two-stepping to round 'em all up in one spot. If you're staying at a hotel in town, I'll see what I can put together and give you a call.''

She opened the door to her Jeep and leaned inside. When she turned back, she had a notepad and pen in hand. ''I'm not staying at a hotel,'' she told him, as she jotted down a series of numbers. ''I have a travel trailer parked on the south side of town.'' She tore the page from the pad and thrust it at him. ''This is my cell number. I answer it twenty-four/seven.''

Rory looked at the number, then over at her, struggling to keep the irritation from his voice. ''Got a name to go with this number?''

''Macy,'' she replied as she climbed back into her Jeep. ''Macy Keller.''

Rory didn't waste any time getting in touch with his brothers. The dust hadn't settled from the Jeep's exit before he was striding to his truck and retrieving his own cell phone from its console. He called Ace first, figuring, as the official head of the family and the one who lived the farthest away, Ace deserved the courtesy.

"We may have us some trouble," he said as soon as he heard his brother's voice.

"Trouble?" Ace repeated.

Scowling, Rory dragged a hand over his sweat-dampened hair. "Yeah. There was a woman just here. At the store. Stopped because she saw the Tanner name on the sign. Said she was looking for Buck."

"Buck? Did she say why?"

Rory huffed a breath. "Said it was none of my business. I told her he'd died last fall. Now she wants to talk to his family. I didn't bother to tell her I was a Tanner. Didn't like her attitude. Plus, I figured whatever business she had with Buck would best be presented to us as a group."

"Damn," Ace swore.

"My sentiments exactly. I told her I'd get in touch with the family and arrange a meeting. Short notice, I know, but is there any way you could come to the ranch tonight? I figure the sooner we find out what she wants, the better."

"Amen to that. Have you talked to the others?"

"No. You're the first I called."

"Call the rest and tell 'em to be at the ranch by eight. I can make it by then if I leave now."

"Consider it done," Rory replied, then broke the connection. He fished the scrap of paper from his pocket, intending to call Macy Keller and tell her he'd set up a meeting for eight that night, then thought better of it, remembering that he'd told her it would take some fancy two-stepping to put this together.

Better to wait a couple of hours before calling her, he decided. Otherwise she might become suspicious and start asking a lot of questions. Like his name.

Chuckling, he stuffed the slip of paper back into his pocket. And he didn't want to tell her his name over the phone. When she discovered who he was, he wanted to be standing opposite her so that he could see the look on her face when she realized that the man who had arranged the meeting for her was none other than Rory Tanner, Buck's youngest son.

As he passed through the gates of the Bar-T, Rory checked his rearview mirror, to make sure the Jeep was still behind him. It was a toss-up as to whether he was relieved or irritated when he saw that it was.

"Insisting on following in her own vehicle," he muttered under his breath. What did she take him for, anyway? A molester? He snorted a breath. Fat chance of him making a move on her. He'd rather cozy up to a patch of poison ivy than cuddle with the likes of her.

Though he had to admit she looked a sight better than she had that afternoon.

She'd traded the overalls and tank top for tan linen trousers and a sleeveless linen blouse a shade or two lighter than the slacks. Still couldn't tell beans about her figure, though, he thought, frowning, as he turned his gaze back to the road. Other than the fact that God had shortchanged her when He was passing out breasts. The woman appeared to be as flat as a pancake.

As he approached the house, he did a quick count of the vehicles that lined the driveway and was relieved to see that all his brothers were present and accounted for. He parked beside Woodrow's wife's car and climbed down from his truck. He waited for Macy to join him, then opened a hand in invitation, indicating for her to proceed him up the walk. At the front door, he reached around her and pushed it open, without bothering to knock.

At her incredulous look, he said, "It's okay. They're expecting us."

Once inside, he didn't waste any time but strode straight for the study, where he found his brothers waiting. Conversation died, as Macy stepped in behind him.

"Macy Keller," he said, beginning the introductions, "these are the Tanners. That's Ace, the oldest, behind the desk. The pretty lady standing beside him is his wife, Maggie, and that's Laura, their daughter, she's holding, who also happens to be Buck's daughter."

At her confused look, he shrugged. "Long story. The short of it is Ace and Maggie adopted Buck's daughter after Buck died." He gestured toward the sofa. "The big, ugly one there is Woodrow and beside him, his wife, Dr. Elizabeth Tanner. Sitting next to Elizabeth is Kayla, the newest member of the Tanner family, and next to her is her husband Dr. Ry Tanner, the second born." He angled his body and waved a hand toward the far wall where a man stood off by himself. "And the lone wolf over there in the corner is Whit. He's a stepbrother and likes to think that makes him different from the others, but it doesn't. He's a Tanner, just like the rest of us."

A choked sound came from beside him. "Us?" she repeated.

It was the moment Rory had waited for. Prepared to enjoy it, he offered her a smile and his hand. "Rory Tanner, ma'am. The youngest son of Buck Tanner."

She folded her arms across her breasts, refusing to shake. "You could've told me that you were a Tanner," she said, her voice sharp with accusation.

"Could've," he agreed, then widened his smile. "But then you never asked, did you?" He gestured toward a chair. "Have a seat."

She jutted her chin. "No thank you. This won't take long." Crossing to the desk, she pulled an envelope from her feed-bucket-style purse and tossed it onto the desktop in front of Ace. "I had planned to give this to Buck. As his oldest son, I assume you're executor of his estate and will know what to do with it."

Ace picked up the envelope and held it up to the light, then glanced at her with a frown. "Looks like there's a check inside."

"There is," she assured him. "A cashier's check in the amount of $75,000."

His frown deepening, he reared back in his chair. "And does this check come with an explanation?"

"I'm returning what's his."

He snorted a breath. "Sorry, but you're going to have to do better than that."

Intrigued by this unexpected turn of events, Rory slid onto a chair, keeping his gaze on Macy's back. The woman was carrying a good-size chip around. Stiff shoulders. Hands clenched into fists at her sides.

If she were wound up any tighter, he figured she'd snap right in two.

"Buck set up a trust for me," she said, then gestured to the envelope. "I'm giving the money back."

"That's a good start, but I think we need to hear the whole story."

She balled her hands into tighter fists. "What exactly is it you want to know?"

Ace tossed the envelope onto the desk. "All of it. You can start with why Buck would feel the need to set up a trust for you."

Her jaw hardened. "Because he thought he was my father."

Ace lifted a brow. "*Thought* he was?"

She gave her chin a tight jerk of acknowledgment.

"And why would Buck think such a thing, if it wasn't the case?"

"Because my mother told him that she was pregnant and that the baby was his."

"Your mother lied?"

She set her teeth so hard, Rory was sure he heard them grind together.

"Yes."

"And you were aware of this lie?"

"No. Growing up, I thought Buck *was* my father."

"And when did you realize that he wasn't?"

"A couple of months ago. My mother told me. I suppose she wanted to clear her conscience." She dropped her chin to her chest and shot a hand beneath her nose. "She was dying."

"This trust Buck set up," Ace continued. "Had you spent the money prior to learning that he wasn't your father?"

She snapped up her head to glare at him. "What does that have to do with anything? I'm giving the money back, aren't I?"

"*If* we choose to accept it," he informed her.

"Why wouldn't you?" she cried. "It was Buck's and given to me under duress, I'm sure. All I want to do is give the money back. Make things right."

"Whatever his reason," Ace said stubbornly, "Buck felt an obligation to set up a trust in your name." He leaned to push the envelope across the desk. "The money is rightfully yours. It has nothing to do with me or my brothers."

She tucked her hands behind her and backed away. "No. I came here to return it and I have. As far as I'm concerned, the slate's clean."

"But—"

She held up a hand, cutting Ace off. "The money isn't mine. It belongs to y'all. You're Tanners, and I'm not."

Before anyone could stop her, she turned and strode from the room. The slam of the front door echoed through the house, confirming her departure.

For a moment, silence reigned in the study.

Frowning, Ace scraped the envelope from the top of the desk and stood. "Well, what do y'all make of *that?*"

Woodrow released the breath he'd been holding. "Beats the hell out of me," he said, then looked around. "But it looks to me like we've come out of this little skirmish with our hair and hide still intact."

His frown deepening, Ace tapped the edge of the envelope against the palm of his hand. "I don't know that we're out of it, yet."

"What do you mean?" Woodrow asked in puzzlement. "The lady admitted that Buck isn't her father, gave the trust money back and hightailed it out of here, asking for nothing. Seems like we ought to be thanking our lucky stars she didn't demand a full share of the estate. She might've, you know."

"Yeah," Ace agreed, nodding. "She might've." He tossed the envelope down on the desk and added grimly, "And that's what has me worried. Why didn't she?"

Rory looked around the room at the others and saw the same doubt mirrored on the faces of the others. "Because she's honest?" he offered. "Because she was trying to right a wrong?"

Ace dragged a hand over his hair, then shook his head. "Maybe. But what if that wasn't her goal? What if she has something else planned? Maybe this deathbed confession of her mother's she told us about was a lie. Maybe she's returning the $75,000 because she's wanting to stake a claim on the old man's estate."

"There's no sense in looking for trouble," Ry said. "Trouble has a habit of finding the Tanners all on its own."

"Better to be prepared for it, then let it catch us unaware," Ace argued.

Maggie stepped forward and laid a supportive hand on her husband's shoulder. "I think Ace is right. Think about it. What woman in her right mind would willingly hand over $75,000 that no one knew she had in the first place?"

"An honest one?" Rory suggested again.

"Do you know that the woman is honest?" Ace asked him in frustration.

Scowling, Rory hunched his shoulders and slid farther down in his chair. "You know damned good and well I don't. She showed up this afternoon at the store out of the blue. I've never seen her before in my life."

"She looked as if she was crying when she left."

Rory snapped his head around to peer at Elizabeth, who had made the remark. "Macy was cryin'?"

Elizabeth nodded. "I would swear I saw tears in her eyes as she ran past."

Rory bolted for the door and outside, stopping on the front porch and watching the cloud of dust that Macy's Jeep had left behind. Frowning, he returned to the study.

"Too late," he informed the others. "She's gone."

"Did she say where she was from?" Ace asked him.

Rory lifted a shoulder as he sank back down on the chair. "She's not much on small talk. All I know is she has a travel trailer parked on a lot south of town."

"If she's parked a trailer, it sounds as if she is planning on hanging around for a while." Ace pursed his lips thoughtfully. "I think we need to keep an eye on her. See what she's up to."

"And how the hell are we supposed to do that?" Rory asked in exasperation.

"One of us needs to befriend her," Ace said. "Find out if she's planning on hanging around and, if she is, why."

"And which one of us have you pegged to play watchdog?" Rory asked dryly. When Ace merely looked at him, Rory glanced around the room and found every pair of eyes focused on him. He shot from his chair. "Uh-uh. No way. I'm not spying on that woman."

"No one is asking you to spy on her," Ace told him. "All we're asking is that you make friends with her. Find out what her plans are."

"Why me?" Rory cried. "Why not one of the others?"

Ace lifted his hands. "You're the logical choice. You're in town every day."

"So is Ry," Rory reminded him.

"Ry's a married man. If he were to befriend the woman, people would talk."

"What about Whit?" Rory asked, desperate to find an alternative. "He's not married."

Whit peeled his back from the wall, his face turning a sickly white. "Oh, no, Ace, please," he begged. "You know how I am around women. I get all tongue-tied and embarrassed. She wouldn't give me the time of day."

Rory spun away in frustration, knowing what Whit said was true. "Man, this is so unfair," he complained.

Grinning, Woodrow stretched out a leg and gave Rory a nudge with the toe of his boot. "Since when do you consider courting a woman as drudgery?"

"*Woman* being the operative word," Rory muttered darkly. "Macy Keller may be a female, but there's not a womanly thing about her."

Scowling, he rammed his hat over his head. "I don't know why I'm the one who gets stuck with all the crummy jobs," he grumbled as he turned for the door. Reaching it, he turned and aimed a warning finger at his brothers. "But I'm telling you right here and now, paybacks are going to be a bitch."

Biting back a smile, Ace crossed the room and handed him the check. "You'll need to return this to her," he said, then gave Rory a confident pat on the back. "I've got faith in you, bro. You can handle this."

"Yeah, yeah," Rory grumbled as he stuffed the check into his wallet. "You're just saying that because you know damn good and well I always get stuck doing the jobs nobody else wants to do."

The rear wheels of Macy's Jeep spewed rock and dust as she shot out onto the highway, anxious to leave the Tanners' ranch behind. She couldn't believe that they'd tried to make her keep the money. What were they? Crazy? Or maybe they were just a bunch of masochists, who enjoyed watching a person suffer.

It wasn't bad enough that she'd had to stand there, like a convicted felon, and admit that her mother had lied to their father. Oh, no, she thought, tightening her hands in a stranglehold on the steering wheel, as the humiliation burned through her again. They'd made her tell the whole embarrassing story, then refused to accept the money, the only way left to her to clear her conscience and right an old wrong.

She narrowed her eyes at the road ahead, her humiliation segueing to fury, as she thought of the cowboy who had offered to arrange the meeting for her in the first place. He'd lied to her. Deceived her. Flirted with her even. And without ever bothering to tell her that he was Buck Tanner's son.

And he'd enjoyed the deception, she thought resentfully. She'd seen the smirk on his face when he'd offered her his hand and introduced himself as "Rory Tanner, Buck Tanner's youngest son."

She shot a hand beneath her eyes, swiping at the tears that leaked onto her cheeks. He had what she'd yearned for, wept over for years. They all did. The Tanner name. But all the years of yearning for the name, while despising the man who had denied her of it, had been for naught. She wasn't a Tanner.

She didn't know who she was.

Two

Ace was trying his best to burn up Rory's cell phone, but Rory was having no part of it. Thanks to the caller ID feature, he knew each time it was Ace who called and refused to answer. He knew what his brother wanted. He was calling to check up on him, make sure that he'd made contact with the Tanners' latest potential nightmare, Macy Keller.

But Rory hadn't done anything about Macy, yet. Couldn't bring himself to dial her cell phone number. What the hell would he say to her if he did? *Hey, it's Rory. The guy who played you for a fool yesterday? I was just wondering if you were planning on doing anything malicious or underhanded to the Tanners.*

He snorted a breath. Yeah. Like the woman was going to tell him if she did have something up her sleeve.

He heaved a weary sigh. But the job of keeping an eye on her was his to do, and he'd do it.

Dammit.

A giant dose of castor oil would go down easier than the thought of striking up a friendship with her. In his estimation, the woman had the hide of a porcupine and the temperament of a grizzly, two traits that any man with half a brain would steer clear of. Though he considered himself an accomplished flirt and possessed an encyclopedia-size repertoire of pickup lines, he couldn't think of a one that would work on this particular female.

Praying he'd be struck with a conversation opener on the drive to the south part of town, he climbed into his truck and pulled out into traffic. He'd made it halfway around the square when he spotted her dust-encrusted Jeep parked in front of the public library. He quickly whipped his truck into the empty space beside it, parked and waited, wondering what in the hell she was doing in the library. Joining the Summer Reading Club?

He'd about decided she had taken up residence inside, when the door to the library opened and she stepped out into the sunshine. She paused to push on her sunglasses, then started down the steep stone steps, her shoulders slumped in dejection, which struck him as odd. What would be disappointing about a trip to the library? Had she been denied a library card? Granted, she wasn't a resident of Tanner's Crossing, but if she'd wanted to check out a book, surely the librarian, Miss Mamie, would've made an exception. Miss Mamie encouraged reading and wouldn't hesitate to bend a few rules to promote it.

Macy was halfway down the steps when he realized that if he didn't hustle, he was going to lose the element of surprise that he needed to corner her.

He quickly hopped down from his truck and propped a hip against the hood of her Jeep.

"Well, fancy meeting you here," he drawled.

She glanced up at the sound of his voice, then flattened her lips in irritation and marched toward him. "That's my Jeep you're sitting on."

He glanced back, as if to verify her claim. "So it is."

She waved an impatient hand. "You can cut the innocent act. What is it you want?"

"Out of life in general?" He reached to thread a strand of hair behind her ear, then met her gaze again, his lips curving in a slow, sensual smile. "Or from a sexy lady like yourself?"

Scowling, she batted his hand away. "Give it up, Romeo. That lady-killer act is wasted on me."

He pressed a palm to his chest. "Why, if I didn't know better, I'd think you didn't like me."

She turned and strode to the driver's side of the Jeep. "I don't."

He pushed away from her hood and followed, wounded, but not ready to give up. "How can you not like me? You don't even know me."

She pulled out her key ring and punched the lock release. "I don't have to. I know your type."

When she reached for the door, he flattened a hand against it, keeping her from opening it. "And what type is that?"

She drew in an angry breath and spun to face him. "A flirt."

Instead of backing off, as she obviously expected him to do, he leaned back against the door and crossed his legs at the ankles, his stance relaxed, friendly. "That's odd. Most women find me irresistible."

"Really?" she said, feigning surprise, then clamped her jaw down in a scowl. "Well, I happen to think you're obnoxious and deceitful, which nixes any chance of me ever liking you, so why don't you quit wasting your time and mine, and get the heck out of my way."

He shook his head with regret. "And here I was about to invite you to dinner."

"I'd starve before I'd go out with you."

He lifted a brow. "You might want to hear where I was planning on taking you before you decide. Bubba's Joint," he continued, not giving her time to tell him the place didn't matter. "Bubba's a legend around here. Stands six-and-a-half-feet tall, weighs a good three hundred pounds and serves up the best barbecue brisket in this part of the country.

"Pecan-smoked," he added. "Which is a tradition in Bubba's family. That would be the McHeeleys. They've lived in Tanner's Crossing almost as long as the Tanners and have always run a restaurant of one sort or another. Usually barbecue. People come from miles around to eat at Bubba's. It takes weeks just to get a reservation." He buffed his nails on the front of his shirt, then held them out to admire. "Of course, if you know the right people, you don't need a reservation."

She folded her arms over her chest and gave him a bored look. "And I suppose you're one of those people."

He shot her a grin. "And here I was thinking you were slow. Fact is, Bubba and me, we go way back. Used to go dove hunting together when we were kids. All I gotta do is pick up the phone and we've got us a prime booth in front of the picture window that looks out over the Lampasas River." He looked down his nose at her, as if he were about to share something of great import. "And let me tell you, there's not a prettier spot on this earth than the Lampasas River at sunset."

He smoothed a hand across the air, as if preparing to paint her a picture. "Water as clear as glass. The sun like a ribbon of fire on its surface. Trees with trunks as thick as a man's chest growing along the jagged cliffs of its banks, their limbs hanging so low, they look like fingers reaching down to dip into the water." He dropped his hand and shot her a wink. "It's a sight to see, and that's a fact."

"Too bad I'll miss it." She flapped an impatient hand. "Now, if you don't mind, I have things to do."

"I swear you're determined to break my heart right in two."

"I'd worry, if I thought you had one."

He staggered, clutching at his chest. "I hope you know CPR," he gasped. "'Cause this heart you don't believe I have just suffered a fatal blow."

"That was your ego," she said dryly. "Not your heart."

Scowling, he straightened. "What is it with you, anyway? I'm just trying to be nice."

"Why?"

He tossed up his hands in frustration. "A guy has to have a reason to be nice to a lady?"

When she merely looked at him, he heaved a sigh, having to dig deep for the patience he was going to need to deal with her. "Look. I don't know you and you don't know me, but obviously, from what you've told us, your mother and my father had some kind of history. I'm just extending you the welcoming hand of friendship out of respect to our deceased parents."

"Whatever relationship our parents had ended years ago and has absolutely nothing to do with either of us. I've returned the money your father gave me, so there's nothing more for us to discuss."

"That remains to be seen."

She narrowed an eye. "And what's that supposed to mean?"

"It *means*," he said, managing to hold on to his temper by a thread. "That if your only reason in coming to Tanner's Crossing was to return the money, you'd be gone by now, as you've already done that. Yet, here you are, still hanging around town."

"Not that it's any of your business," she informed him tersely, "but returning the money wasn't my only reason for coming to Tanner's Crossing. Up until two months ago, I thought Buck Tanner was my father. Now that I know he wasn't, I intend to find out who is." She gave him an angry shove, wrenched open the door and climbed inside. "And whether you like it or not, I'm staying in Tanner's Crossing until I do."

"Whoa," he said, catching the door before she could slam it in his face. "Are you saying that you don't know who your father is?"

"That's exactly what I'm saying," she snapped. "Now, if you don't mind..."

She gave the door a yank, but Rory stubbornly held on. There were tears in her eyes, but he could tell she wasn't going to let them fall. Not in front of him.

"You said your mother died," he said, trying to sort all the facts in his head. "So obviously she either didn't want you to know who your father was or died before she could tell you." He looked at her closely, trying to decide which was the case. He found the answer in her eyes. "She didn't want you to know," he said slowly, seeing the hurt there.

Turning her face away, she thrust the key into the ignition and started the engine. "Nice work, Sherlock. Now, unless you want to lose that arm, I'd advise you to let go of my door."

Instead of releasing it, Rory moved in closer. "That's what you were doing in the library, wasn't it? You were searching for clues to your father's identity. Probably going through old newspapers, looking for mentions of your mother, in hopes of finding a lead."

"You're a regular detective, aren't you? Unfortunately, my mother wasn't the type whose activities were recorded in the society section."

"Have you talked to your brothers or sisters about this? Maybe your mother told them more than she did you."

She snorted a breath. "I would've if I had any. My mother didn't want children, including me."

"So what are you going to do now?"

She tightened her hands on the steering wheel, her determination obvious in her white-knuckled grip.

"Check the county records. Talk to people. Some-one's bound to know something."

"I hope you're not counting on anyone in Tanner's Crossing telling you anything."

Her eyes sharpened at the warning, then narrowed suspiciously. "Why wouldn't they?"

"This is a small town. People here are a tight-knit group, who protect their own. A stranger comes into town and starts asking a lot of questions about the past…" He lifted his hands, as if the answer was obvious. "They aren't going to tell you what you want to know."

He'd no sooner offered the explanation, than Rory realized that he'd just stumbled upon the excuse he needed to keep an eye on her.

"I could help you," he offered. "I'm a Tanner. Grew up here. People trust me. My name alone will open doors that would get slammed in your face, if you were to try this on your own."

She hesitated a moment, her brow pleated, as if considering his offer. Then she gave him a push that sent him stumbling back clear of the door. "Nice try, Romeo," she muttered. "But I don't want or need your help."

Rolling his eyes skyward, Rory pressed the receive button on his cell phone and brought it to his ear. "Yes, Ace, I talked to her," he said without pream-ble.

"How'd you know it was me calling?"

Rory signaled the UPS driver to stack the boxes by the door. "I'm psychic." He quickly counted the boxes, then scrawled his name across the invoice, acknowledging receipt. "And because I'm psychic," he said into the receiver, "I also know what you want and the answer is, yes. I talked to Macy, and she says the reason she's staying here is to find her real father."

"Do you believe her?"

Rory lifted a hand in farewell to the driver, then frowned, turning his full attention to the call. "You're awfully damn suspicious."

"Cautious," Ace corrected. "When we're dealing with anything associated with the old man, caution is always the best course."

Dragging a weary hand over his hair, Rory sank down on a box. "I see your point."

"So you're planning to continue to keep an eye on her, right?"

"Do I have a choice?"

"No."

Rory heaved a sigh. "Then, yeah, I guess I am."

Macy wrapped her arms around the steering wheel and dropped her head against its center. Two days digging through court records and trying to get people to talk to her and she'd come up with nothing. Nada. A big fat zero.

Lifting her head, she propped her chin on her hands and stared glumly out the windshield. She hated to admit it, but it appeared that Rory Tanner was right. The citizens of Tanner's Crossing weren't going to share any secrets about their townspeople with a stranger. She needed help.

Unfortunately the only person she knew to ask for that help was Rory, and she'd rather eat brussels sprouts—her least favorite vegetable—than ask him for anything. He might be a Matthew McConaughey look-alike, with his chiseled features and lady-killer grin, but whatever attraction she might have felt for him ended when he'd failed to tell her he was a Tanner. And he'd enjoyed the deception. She could still see the smug look on his face when he'd stuck out his hand and introduced himself as "Rory Tanner, Buck Tanner's youngest son," succeeding in humiliating her in front of his entire family.

But he'd offered her his help, she reminded herself.

And she'd slam-dunked his offer right back in his face.

With a groan, she started the Jeep's engine and backed out of the parking space, certain that he would never agree to assist her after the way she'd treated him. But with no other options open to her, she was willing to get down on her hands and knees and beg, if necessary, to get him to reconsider his offer.

At the four-way stop that marked the northwest corner of the square, she pulled into a space on the lot adjacent to Tanner's Cowboy Outfitters and parked. A quick scan of the area revealed pallets of grass, positioned randomly around the parking lot, and about ten twelve-foot rows of potted plants and shrubs, all of which were wilting under a hot midday sun. She spotted Rory immediately, standing in front of his store, his back to her, a cell phone at his ear. She didn't have to hear his conversation to know that he was mad. *Really* mad, if body language was any indication. He stood with his legs braced wide, his shoulders squared, as if ready for a fight.

Though she'd never admit it to anyone, least of all

Rory Tanner, who obviously already possessed a Texas-size ego, he could've played the starring role in a fantasy she'd indulged in as a teenager. A rough-and-tumble cowboy, riding in to rescue her from a life that her mother had made a living hell. He'd hold her mother and stepfather off at gunpoint, swing her up onto the saddle behind him, then ride away into the sunset, where she'd live the kind of life she'd always yearned for.

Probably a result of watching too many Western movies on late-night television, she thought wryly, and made herself focus on the purpose of her visit.

Bracing herself for what she feared was going to be a humbling experience, she climbed down from her Jeep and strode purposefully toward Rory. She was less than ten feet away, when he yelled at the top of his lungs, ''I don't care what that lying son of a bitch says! I've got a contract with his name on it that says he's doing this landscaping job. You find him and tell him to get his butt over here and I mean *now!*''

He held the phone to his ear a moment longer, obviously listening, then reared back and hurled it through the air, swearing a blue streak.

Stunned, Macy stumbled to a stop and watched as the phone struck the store's stone front with a *whack* and exploded, sending shards of debris flying in every direction.

His shoulders rigid in anger, he wheeled but skidded to a stop when he saw her. ''What the hell do you want?'' he snapped.

Maybe this isn't the best time to ask for a favor, she thought weakly. She took another quick look at the plants withering beneath the hot sun, and decided he might be more amenable to a trade than a favor. It was certainly more appealing to her than getting down on her knees and begging.

She slid her hands into the pockets of her slacks, trying for a casual nonchalance. "Sounds as if your landscaper didn't show up."

His lip curled in a snarl at the mention of the landscaper. "The swindler thinks a week-long vacation in the Bahamas is more important than honoring a signed contract."

"That's too bad," she said, and started down a narrow aisle created by rows of plants. "Better get some water on these," she warned, brushing her fingertips along leaves already beginning to droop. "These plants are going to die in this heat if they aren't put in the ground soon."

She heard the stomp of his footsteps behind her but kept walking.

"I'm aware of that," he growled, "and I intend to see what I can do about it, just as soon as I get rid of you."

She stooped to right a fallen pot. "I could do the landscape job for you."

There was a moment of stunned silence, then his strangled *"You?"*

Irritated that he'd doubt her ability, she shot him a frown. "Yes, me." Keeping the frown, she squatted down to examine a red yucca plant. "If you're worried that I'd botch the job, there's no need. I've had plenty of experience."

"Doing what? Puttering around in a flower bed in your backyard?" He snorted a laugh. "Lady, this is

about ten hours of backbreaking work, and that's if
you had a crew helping you.''

She stood and dusted off her hands. ''I'd imagine
I could scrape together a crew. Most towns usually
have a place where day laborers can be hired.''

He looked at her more closely. ''Are you serious
about this?''

''Yes, I am.''

He dragged a hand over his mouth, considering.
''And how much would you charge me to do the
job?''

''The only money you'd be out would be for the
day laborers I hire. We can work a trade for my fee.''

''And what kind of trade did you have in mind?''

''I'll do your landscaping and you'll help me find
my father.''

''Ah,'' he said, lifting a brow as understanding
dawned. ''I take it you've had a few doors slammed
in your face.''

It was so like him to rub it in her face. ''A few,''
she admitted reluctantly.

''I'd say 'I told you so,' but I'm too much of a
gentleman to stoop that low.''

''A gentleman wouldn't have brought it up in the
first place.''

Smiling, he extended his hand. ''Gentleman or not,
you've got yourself a deal. When can you start?''

She eyed his hand a moment, wary, but told herself
the shake was necessary to seal the agreement. Grabbing his hand, she gave it a quick pump, then dropped
it and turned for her Jeep, wiping her palm down her
thigh.

"I'll be back as soon as I can put together a crew," she called over her shoulder. "Shouldn't take me long."

It was a good thing Rory wasn't a gambling man. He'd have bet the ranch that he wouldn't see Macy again for days, if at all. He would have lost the bet—and the ranch—because, within the hour, she was back, her Jeep loaded down with men and equipment.

Unable to believe she'd pulled it off, he stepped outside his store and watched as she began dragging tools out of the back of her Jeep and passing them out to the men lined up, waiting. He noted that she was dressed in overalls and a tank top again, which he was beginning to believe was her standard wear. A ball cap covered her hair, its brim pulled down low to shade her face from the sun. Sunglasses shielded her eyes and a pair of beat-up running shoes peeked from beneath the hems of her overalls.

Once the tools were distributed, she motioned for the men to follow her to a pallet of grass, where she gave clipped orders in Spanish, instructing the men to rake the ground smooth and lay out the sod. Once she was sure they'd understood her instructions, she pulled a clipboard from the front seat of her Jeep and headed for the rows of potted plants. With the clipboard braced against her middle, she studied the site a moment, then bent her head and began to write.

Curious to see what she was up to, Rory moved to peer over her shoulder. "What are you doing?"

She jumped, then frowned and angled her body away from him. "Drawing a design."

"You're an artist?"

"No. A landscape architect."

He drew back to frown at the back of her head. "You didn't say anything about being a landscape architect."

"Kinda like you not saying anything about being a Tanner?" she asked, then gave him a smug two-can-play-this-game smile, tucked the clipboard beneath her arm and strode for the front of the building.

Score one for the lady, he thought in grudging admiration, then followed.

When he caught up with her, she was studying the building, her lips pursed in concentration. After a moment, she lifted the clipboard, flipped a page and began to sketch again.

He watched in fascination as a rough but amazingly detailed drawing of his store appeared on the blank page. "You're really good at that," he said, surprised at her skill.

Her attention focused on her work, she murmured a distracted "I get by."

"Was that part of your training?"

She glanced up at him in confusion. "What?"

He gestured toward the clipboard. "Drawing."

She resumed her sketching. "Yes and no. Yes, we were required to draw structures to scale, and no, there were no formal classes in which we were taught artistic technique."

Catching her lower lip between her teeth, she tapped the end of the pencil against the drawing. "There isn't room for structured beds," she said, as if thinking aloud. "But the front needs color and softening. I'd suggest some potted plants. A whiskey barrel or two here," she said, and quickly sketched them into the design. "A horse trough would work beneath the display windows,'' she added, drawing it in, as well. ''Plus it would add character and offer an element of authenticity to the store. We could fill it with seasonal flowers. Geraniums in the summer and pansies in the winter. Or, if you'd prefer, we could plant succulents that could stay year-round.

''And along this side of the property,'' she said, using the pencil to point at the narrow strip of land between his and the neighboring business, ''we could plant ornamental trees. Texas mountain laurels would do well there. There's adequate sunlight and room for them to grow. Or, if you'd rather have more color, we could use crepe myrtles. Both would offer privacy and enhance the aesthetics of your store.''

Rory gave his head a shake, amazed at how quickly she had put together what looked like an inspired design. ''Wow. You're good at this. Really good.''

Putting the pencil to paper again, she scribbled notes in the margin. ''Your father paid for my education. The money wasn't wasted, although I did pay it back.''

''Speaking of that,'' he said, and pulled his wallet from his back pocket. He drew out the cashier's check and held it out to her. ''This is yours. My brothers and I agree that you should keep it.''

She looked at the check, then turned away, tucking the clipboard under her arm. ''I don't want it.''

Frustrated, Rory followed. ''There's no use arguing over this. We don't want or need the money. Besides, Buck gave it to you.''

''Under duress,'' she reminded him.

''Macy—''

She spun to face him, her mouth set in a deter-

mined line. "Look. I didn't like your father. I didn't
know him, but I didn't like him, which I think is
understandable, considering he chose to set up a trust
fund for me, rather than raise me as his own child.
Then I learned that he wasn't my father. That I'd
hated and resented an innocent man for years. That
I'd been used as an unknowing pawn to milk him for
money. Do you know how that makes me feel?" Setting her jaw, she turned away. "Rotten. That's how.
Giving the money back is the only way I have to
make it up to him, to right a wrong."

The woman felt guilty for thinking mean thoughts
about Buck? Rory would've laughed, but he had a
feeling she wouldn't understand the humor, even if
he cared to explain it to her.

"Tell you what," he said, moving around her. He
made a show of slipping the check back into his wallet and the wallet into the pocket of his jeans. "We'll
table this for now." When she would've argued, he
held up a hand. "I understand your reasons for wanting to give the money back, but you've got to understand my brothers' and my position, as well. Whatever his reasons in doing so, it was Buck who gave
you the money and we don't feel it's our place to
take it back. And as to you feeling guilty about re-
senting Buck—" He paused and scratched his jaw.
"Well, if it'll make you feel any better, my brothers
and I didn't like him much, either."

Her eyes widened in surprise. "You didn't?"

"Nope, and for much the same reason as you. The
old man may have claimed us, but he was never much
of a father."

* * *

The next afternoon, Rory stood before the front window of his store, looking out. Country-western music pulsed around him from speakers set strategically throughout the store. Behind him, his staff laughed and talked as they priced merchandise and put it out for display in preparation for the grand opening, a week away. Beyond the window, Macy strolled around the perimeter of the parking lot, inspecting the completed landscaping job, pausing occasionally to pinch off a dead bloom or tamp down loose mulch around a plant.

He couldn't believe she'd managed to pull it off. And the design she'd come up with was a sight better than the one the original landscaper had proposed for the job…and cheaper, too, considering she was trading her own fee for his help in finding her father.

Man, that's got to be tough, he thought, thinking about what she'd told him. Not knowing who your father was. He supposed, now that he thought about it, it might explain why she walked around with her shoulders hunched up close to her ears. That chip she carried was quite a load for anyone to haul around, much less a woman.

She glanced toward the store and their gazes met. He felt a jolt to his system at the contact and was a little unnerved by it, as it was one he usually attributed to sexual interest. But he wasn't attracted to her, he told himself. Hell, just look at her! With that ball cap turned around backward on her head and her overalls splattered with mud, she looked more like a twelve-year-old boy than she did a woman.

He hauled in a deep breath to ward off the panic

that wanted to grab him by the throat and told himself it was pity he felt for her. Yeah, pity, he thought, going almost weak with relief that he'd identified the emotion.

She motioned for him to come outside and he lifted a hand in acknowledgment, then headed for the door. "I'm calling it a day," he called to his staff. "If you need me, you can reach me on my cell."

"You busted your cell phone."

He paused in the doorway to look back at his manager, Linda Sue Carmichael, a woman in her mid-fifties and a family friend who went back years. Grinning, he shot her a wink. "Don't worry that pretty little head of yours. I already bought another one. Same number," he added as he let the door close behind him.

Shoving his hands into his pockets, he strode toward Macy, who waited beneath the scrap of shade created by one of the mountain laurels she'd planted.

"All done?" he called to her.

She nodded, then gestured toward the men waiting beside her Jeep. "All that's left is paying the men."

"How much?"

She named a figure, and Rory pulled out his wallet. He peeled off several bills, then slipped the wallet back into his pocket.

She quickly counted the money, then passed back one of the bills. "You gave me a hundred too much."

He waved her away. "It's for the men. Tell 'em it's a bonus for all their hard work." He hitched his hands low on his hips and looked around, pleased with the results. "You did a good job, Macy. And I don't mind telling you, it looks a hell of a lot better than Arnold could've done.''

She stuffed the wad of bills into her pocket. ''I'll tell the men you're pleased with their work.''

''And *yours*,'' he said, giving her a pointed look. ''The design is what makes the difference.''

She shrugged. ''A design isn't worth squat if not properly implemented. The men worked hard and followed instructions well. With the proper care, your grass and plants should thrive.''

''They'll get the care they need,'' he assured her.

She shuffled uneasily from one foot to the other, as if she had something to say but was having a hard time spitting it out.

''About your end of our trade,'' she began uneasily.

He held up a hand. ''Say no more. I intend to uphold my end of our bargain. In fact, I've already given this some thought. Buck used to hang out at a place in Killeen called the Longhorn. Dixie Leigh is the owner and a personal friend of the family. I figure we can pay her a visit. See what she knows.''

She took an expectant step toward him. ''Now?''

Wrinkling his nose, he backed away and gave her a slow look down and up. ''You might want to change clothes first.''

She huffed a breath. ''I didn't mean right this minute. I have to take the guys home first. I can meet you back here—'' she glanced at her wristwatch ''—in, say, an hour and a half?''

Rory checked his own watch and nodded. ''Six o'clock, it is.''

* * *

Rory stole a glance at Macy, who rode in the passenger seat next to him. The woman was a bundle of nerves.

"Much more and you're going to twist that necklace in two," he warned.

Startled, she glanced his way, then down to the fingers she had twined through her gold chain. Embarrassed, she unwound her fingers and tucked them beneath her thighs, pinning them against the seat. "Sorry. I guess I'm a little nervous."

"Nothing to be nervous about," he told her as he swung his truck into an empty space in front of the Longhorn and parked. "Dixie Leigh is one of the sweetest ladies I've ever known." He reached for the door handle and glanced her way. "Ready?"

She gulped, nodded, then climbed down.

With Rory leading the way, she followed him into the bar. Though it was nearly seven, the place was almost empty. Two soldiers played a game of eight ball at a pool table, while several cowboys sipped beer from the comfort of a booth near the bar.

But it was early yet. Rory knew from experience that by nine o'clock the place would be hopping, packed tight with cowboys and soldiers, looking for a good time. With that in mind, he guided Macy toward the bar, where a bartender lazily polished a glass.

"Excuse me," he said to the bartender. "Is Dixie around?"

The man shouted over his shoulder, "Hey, Dix! There's a guy here wantin' to see you."

"Tell him I gave at the office!"

The voice came from behind a door marked Office

and was gruff enough to have Macy frowning up at Rory.

"That's what you call *sweet?*" she asked wryly.

Chuckling, he hooked an arm around her waist and headed for the office door. "Don't worry. Dixie's all bark and no bite." He rapped his knuckles against the door. "Hey, Dixie!" he called. "It's me. Rory Tanner."

The door swung wide and a middle-aged woman with fire-engine-red hair appeared in the opening. Dressed in skin-tight jeans and a breasts-hugging T-shirt with Boss Lady emblazoned across its front, she looked more than capable of handling whatever trouble came her way.

Yanking a cigarette from her mouth, she squared off with Rory, as if ready to fight. "Well, you took your dead-easy time gettin' over here. Been home nearly a month and this is the first time I lay eyes on you."

"Now, Dixie," he soothed. "I'd've come sooner, but I've been busy getting the new store ready to open."

She reached up and smacked him upside the head. "Since when is work more important than family?" she snapped. Biting back a smile, she opened her arms. "Come here, you great big hunk of man, and give me a hug."

Macy watched in amazement as, laughing, Rory scooped Dixie up into his arms and twirled her around.

"Put me down, before you make me burn you with my cigarette," she fussed.

Once on her feet again, she snatched her T-shirt

back into place and jerked her chin toward Macy. "Who's the chick?"

"No need to be jealous," Rory teased. "You know my heart belongs to you."

Dixie waved a dismissive hand, leaving a trail of cigarette smoke hanging in the air between them. "Honey, I've spent too many years working in bars to fall for a line of bull like that. So?" she said, and turned, giving Macy a slow look up and down. "You got a name?"

Intimidated but refusing to show it, Macy stuck out a hand. "Macy Keller."

"Keller," Dixie repeated, and eyed Macy curiously as she shook her hand. "That name sure rings a bell. Are you from around here?"

Hope surged through Macy. "No, ma'am. But my mother was. That's why I'm here. I was hoping you might've known her."

Dixie eyed her a moment longer, then sighed. "Better step on inside," she said, gesturing for the two to follow her into her office. "Somethin' tells me we're goin' to want some privacy for this conversation."

Macy and Rory sat down on the tattered sofa opposite Dixie's desk, while Dixie took the chair behind it.

"My mother's name was Darla Jean Keller," Macy began, anxious to get to the point of their visit. "Do you remember her?"

"Darla Jean?" Dixie chuckled. "Lord, yes, I remember her. Pretty girl with champagne taste and a beer pocketbook."

"That would be my mother, all right," Macy said dryly.

Dixie shook a cigarette from a pack, slipped it between her lips, touched a lighter to its end, then reared back in her chair, inhaling deeply. "That Darla Jean was a feisty one. I doubt a weekend passed that she wasn't over here in Killeen at one bar or another. Drew men like flies and didn't mind passing out the honey." She glanced over at Macy, as if fearing she'd offended her.

Though embarrassed by her mother's less-than-sterling reputation, Macy waved a hand, urging her to go on. "No, please. That's why I'm here. I want to know everything you remember about her."

"Why?" Dixie asked bluntly. "The past is the past. Why not let it rest?"

Macy curled her hands into fists against her knees. "Because I'm part of that past. When my mother left Tanner's Crossing twenty-nine years ago, she was pregnant with me." She glanced over at Rory, silently asking his permission to tell it all. At his nod, she turned back to Dixie. "My mother told me that Buck Tanner was my father. I believed he was until a little over two months ago, when she confessed that she'd lied. Not only to me, but to Buck, too. She somehow managed to convince him that the baby she carried was his, thinking he'd marry her. Instead, he bought her off. Gave her money to move away, with the promise that she'd never return to Tanner's Crossing."

Dixie drew on her cigarette thoughtfully, then slowly blew out a stream of smoke. "So now you're wantin' to find out who your real daddy is."

Emotion clotted in Macy's throat. "Yes," she admitted. "And I'm hoping that you can help me."

Dixie stubbed out her cigarette in an ashtray already overflowing with butts, then looked Macy square in the eye. "Honey," she said, "as much as I'd like to help you, I can't. Like I said, your mama drew men like flies. If I was to take a guess which one of 'em fathered you, I might as well hand you the telephone book."

Her heart sinking, Macy dropped her gaze. "I understand." She inhaled a deep breath, then stood and forced a smile. "Thank you for your time, Dixie. I appreciate your willingness to talk to me."

Rory picked up his hat and stood, too. "Yeah, Dix. Thanks."

They'd nearly reached the door when Dixie called out, "Wait a minute."

They both turned to peer at her.

"Your mama had a girlfriend she ran with," she said. "Sheila Tompkins, I think was her name. Haven't seen hide nor hair of Sheila since she and Darla Jean quit coming around here, but if anybody would know Darla Jean's secrets, it would be Sheila. Those two gals were thicker than thieves."

Three

The return trip to Tanner's Crossing was a quiet one. Macy didn't seem in the mood to talk and Rory wasn't about to press her into conversation, fearing she'd burst into tears if he did. She was wound up tighter than a seven-day clock and had been since they'd left the Longhorn. When the spring broke—and there was no doubt in his mind that it would—tears were going to be shed, and he didn't intend to be around to mop up the mess.

He supposed he could understand why she was upset, though. Dixie wasn't one to mince words, and what she'd had to say about Darla Jean Keller hadn't exactly been flattering. A telephone book, he thought, with a woeful shake of his head, remembering Dixie's way of letting Macy know that her mother had slept with a lot of men. He knew it must have been hard for Macy to sit and listen to her mother's reputation discussed so graphically. Even more so to have to hear it in Rory's presence.

But Rory knew what it was like to be ashamed of a parent's actions. It was a miracle he and his brothers could hold their heads up, what with all the shenanigans their old man had pulled. But that was the past, and Rory—as Dixie had suggested Macy do—was satisfied to let it rest.

Macy didn't seem so inclined.

But he supposed he could understand that, too. If he'd spent the better part of his life thinking one man was his father, then learned it wasn't true, he might be as hell-bent as she was to find out who had sired him.

But knowing why Macy was upset and understanding her reasons for being so didn't make the long, silent drive home any more pleasant.

By the time they pulled into the parking lot of Tanner's Cowboy Outfitters, it was just past ten and the square was quiet as a tomb, not a person or vehicle in sight, which wasn't uncommon in Tanner's Crossing, where the streets were all but rolled up at ten.

Rory shut off the ignition and switched off the headlights, throwing the parking lot into darkness. He waited six heartbeats—he knew because he counted every one of 'em—to see who would break the silence. Macy was the first to crack.

"Do you know her?"

He knew without asking who she was talking about. Sheila Tompkins, the woman Dixie had said was her mother's best friend. He shook his head. "No. I'm not familiar with the name."

"Tompkins is probably her maiden name. She would go by her husband's, if she'd married."

"Yeah," he agreed. "I imagine she would." He hesitated a moment, unsure how far she wanted to pursue this, and less sure if he wanted to be involved if she did. "I could ask around," he offered. "See if anybody recognizes the name."

"I'd appreciate that."

She opened her door, but Rory reached across the console and caught her arm, stopping her, before she could climb down. "Are you sure you want to do this? I mean…well, you could be setting yourself up for some major pain by digging up the past."

She glanced back over her shoulder. "If you were in my place, would you quit now?"

Thanks to the interior light he was now able to see her face, and what he saw was enough to make a grown man cry. Her face was pale and taut with emotion, her eyes bright with unshed tears. With a sigh, he released her arm and sank back against the seat. "No, I don't suppose I would."

He watched as she climbed down, fumbling with her keys to unlock her door. He reached for his own keys to start his truck but froze when he heard a choking sound. The dam had finally broken. He knew it as well as he knew his own name. He considered for a moment driving off and leaving her to cry it out alone, but his fingers refused to turn the key.

With a muttered curse, he shouldered open his door and dropped to the ground. Rounding the hood of his truck, he caught her by the elbow and spun her around.

"Come here," he said gruffly, and hauled her up against his chest.

He could tell that she didn't want his comfort. Her body remained as stiff as a poker within the scope of his arms, her hands balled into tight fists against his chest. Yet she didn't try to pull away, which surprised him. She just cried. Great heaving sobs that shook her shoulders and reverberated through his chest, chipping at a heart steeled against compassion. Within seconds his shirt was soaked by her tears, their dampness burning like acid against his skin. Helpless to know what else to do, he cupped a hand behind her neck and drew her head beneath his chin.

She wasn't any bigger than a minute, he thought as he stroked a hand down her back, trying his best to soothe her. He could feel every vertebra, every rib that lay beneath her skin. But he wasn't fool enough to mistake her slenderness as a sign of weakness. She was tough, both in body and spirit. He'd seen her heft five-gallon pots of shrubs and tote 'em around, as if they were filled with nothing but air. And she'd stood up to a roomful of Tanner men, who, when joined, created an intimidating show of force he'd seen more than one man back down from.

As he stroked his hand down her back again, he thought he sensed a relaxing of her body. Once alerted to the change, he became aware of the slow unfurling of her fingers, the splay of her hands, as she opened them over his chest. Her hands, like the rest of her, were slim, delicately formed, yet strong. He wondered what they would feel like on his bare flesh.

A shudder moved through her and he wrapped his arms more tightly around her, gave her a reassuring squeeze. "You okay?" he asked quietly.

Her head bumped his chin in a nod.

He loosened his hold on her to tug a handkerchief from his back pocket, and pressed it into her hand. She stepped from his embrace, holding the wadded handkerchief beneath her nose.

"Do you think you can make it home okay?" he asked.

She nodded but kept her head down, as if embarrassed to look at him.

"I can follow you, if you want," he offered. "Or I could drive you. Your Jeep would be safe here overnight."

She shook her head. "I'm okay." She turned and opened her door, then stopped, her back to him. She drew in a deep, shuddery breath, murmured "Thanks," then quickly climbed into her Jeep and closed the door between them.

Rory stood in the parking lot, watching as she drove away, immobilized by that one word. *Thanks*. Though the word was all but wrung from her, the sincerity in it touched something deep inside him.

He watched until her taillights disappeared from sight, wanting to go after her, thinking she shouldn't be alone. Not when she was feeling so blue.

With a shake of his head, he turned for his truck. Don't let your emotions get involved, he told himself. She was a job his brothers had stuck him with, nothing more. Once she found her father, she'd leave town and his business with her would be over.

Frowning, he stopped at the side of his truck and

rubbed at a dull ache in his chest. Indigestion? he asked himself. He considered a moment, then blew out a breath and climbed inside. Had to be. He sure as hell didn't feel anything for Macy Keller.

Macy lay in the narrow bed in her trailer, her eyes swollen from crying, her throat raw from trying to hold more tears back. To say she was disappointed would be the understatement of the year. She'd had such high hopes that Dixie would be able to name her father.

The woman was certainly a character, she thought, forcing her mind from her disappointment. That bee-hive of flaming red hair, the skin-tight T-shirt and jeans, the ever-present cigarette dangling from the corner of her mouth. And she certainly didn't attempt to whitewash the truth. At first, she'd intimidated Macy. But it didn't take Macy long to realize that what Rory had said was true. Dixie was all bark and no bite.

And she obviously adored Rory.

Macy frowned, remembering the way Rory had scooped Dixie up and swung her around, laughing. Granted, Rory was a flirt. She'd seen evidence enough of that to know it was true. But his affection for Dixie was unquestionably sincere, which made her wonder at the "friend of the family" connection he'd mentioned.

At the reminder of Rory, she inched farther down on the bed and pulled the sheet to her chin, remembering his kindness to her. He'd surprised her when he'd offered her his comfort. She hated the fact that she'd broken down in front of him. Crying revealed weakness and Macy refused to let anyone know her vulnerabilities. Some people, she knew, used any sign of weakness to take advantage of a person, to steamroll them in order to get their way. Macy's mother had done that and Macy refused to allow anyone to hurt her again. Her mother had hurt her enough.

But Rory hadn't seemed to consider her tears as a sign of weakness. He'd seemed only concerned. She shivered, remembering the feel of his arms around her, the sense of security she'd experienced in his embrace, the comfort he'd offered when she'd so desperately needed it. It was silly, she knew, but when he was holding her, she felt as if her fantasy cowboy had ridden onto the scene to rescue her from her misery.

She flopped over onto her side and punched her pillow up beneath her head. And that's ridiculous, she told herself. That was the kind of thinking that got a woman into trouble. Instead of using her own wits to take care of herself, she depended on a man to do the job. That's what Macy's mother had done when she'd married Macy's stepfather. In doing so, she'd shackled herself to a tight-fisted man, more stubborn and selfish than she was and had spent the remainder of her life punishing everyone else for her mistake. Most especially Macy.

Macy flattened her lips in grim determination. She wasn't going to fall into that trap, she told herself. To start depending on Rory Tanner would be a huge mistake. She did things alone, lived alone.

It was the only way she knew to survive.

Since Ry and Kayla's marriage, Sunday dinner at the Bar-T had become a family tradition, one that

Rory looked forward to and rarely missed. But on this particular Sunday, he was running late, thanks to a sleepless night, worrying about one Miss Macy Keller. The woman had enough problems to keep a convent of nuns on their knees for a year.

By the time he strode into the dining room of his family home, his brothers and their wives were already seated. He made a quick sweep around the table, giving his sisters-in-law all a kiss before dropping down into the chair next to his niece's high chair.

"Hey, sugar," he said, and leaned to rub his nose against the baby's. "How's my favorite girl?"

"Don't fall for that line," Ace warned his daughter. "He tells all the ladies they're his favorite."

Chuckling, Rory dragged his napkin over his lap. "Can I help it if I like women?"

"A trait you inherited from the old man," Ace muttered under his breath

"I heard that," Rory said indignantly.

Ace shrugged. "If the shoe fits…"

Seated on Rory's left, Ry shoved a bowl of mashed potatoes into Rory's hands. "Eat," he ordered. "You two can fight it out later."

Scowling, Rory scooped potatoes onto his plate.

"How's the house going?" Ry asked, in an obvious attempt to forestall a war.

Rory lifted a shoulder and passed the bowl on. "It's coming along. I whipped by before coming up to the house and saw that they'd delivered the drywall. Looks like they plan to start hanging it the first of this week."

"I heard that Macy Keller did the landscaping at

your store,'' Woodrow said. ''How'd you swing that?''

Rory scraped some black-eyed peas onto his plate. ''The landscaper I hired to do the job skipped town, so Macy offered to do it.''

''Offered?'' Ace repeated, lifting a brow.

Rory stabbed a piece of meat from a platter and slapped it onto his plate, not yet ready to forgive Ace for the crack he'd made about him inheriting their father's womanizing gene. ''Not that it's any of your business,'' he informed Ace tersely, ''but we made a trade.''

Woodrow snorted a laugh. ''And I'll bet I can guess what Miss Keller got in the trade.''

Rory smirked. ''If your guess involves the letters *S-E-X,* you're dead wrong.''

Woodrow lifted a brow. ''Really? I thought that's how you charmed women into doing things for you.''

''I don't have to charm women into doing anything. They do things for me because they want to.''

Woodrow hid a smile behind his glass of tea. ''And what they want is to get in your pants.''

Rory opened his hands in a helpless gesture. ''Is it my fault women find me irresistible?'' He picked up his fork. ''And just to set the record straight,'' he said, aiming the tines at Ace. ''Macy was the one who set the terms of the trade, not me.''

''So what does she get out of the deal?'' Ace asked.

Proud of the way he'd managed to kill two birds with one stone, Rory scooped up a forkful of potatoes. ''I agreed to help her find her father. Figured it was a good way to keep an eye on her.''

"Good thinking," Ace said in approval. "Have you had any luck finding the man?"

"We paid Dixie a visit last night. She remembered Macy's mother and gave us the name of one of her mother's friends. Sheila Tompkins. Ever heard of her?"

"Tompkins?" Ace repeated, frowning as he played the name through his mind. "Can't say that I have. How about you, Woodrow?"

Woodrow shook his head. "No Tompkins around these parts that I'm aware of."

"Have you checked the telephone directory?" Maggie suggested helpfully.

"None listed." Rory broke off a chunk of roll and tossed it onto the tray of Laura's high chair, grinning as he watched his niece close her chubby fist around it.

Maggie pried the chunk from Laura's hand. "No bread," she ordered sternly, "until she finishes her vegetables."

Rory looked at the blob of green in the bowl on Laura's tray and curled his nose. "You call that vegetables? Looks to me like a pile of fresh cow sh—"

Ace silenced him with a warning look, then tipped his head toward Laura. "Little ears."

"Like she's never heard it from you," Rory grumbled. He scooped up a spoonful of creamed spinach and held it before Laura's mouth. "Come on, sugar," he coaxed. "Eat your spinach and Uncle Rory will give you his roll."

Laura squinched up her face and pushed the spoon away.

"I bet I know who would remember Sheila Tompkins," Elizabeth said.

"Who?" Woodrow asked.

While everyone's attention was diverted, Rory quickly popped the spoonful of spinach into his mouth, wanting to help the kid out. He immediately wished he hadn't.

"Maw Parker," Elizabeth replied, while Rory looked desperately around for someplace to spit the spinach out. "She's lived here forever and knows everyone in town."

"She'd be the one, all right," Woodrow agreed, then turned to Rory. "Why don't you give Maw a call?"

Caught, there was nothing for Rory to do but swallow the slimy mess. Shuddering, he grabbed his glass of tea. "I'll do that," he managed to choke out, before downing half the glass's contents in an effort to wash the awful taste from his mouth.

Elizabeth looked at him curiously. "Are you okay?" she asked in concern.

Rory pressed a hand to his stomach, praying the spinach would stay down. "Yeah. Fine."

"What are your impressions of Macy?" Ace asked curiously.

Rory passed the baby her spoon. "You're on your own kid," he said under his breath, then turned his attention to Ace. "She's all right, I guess. Why?"

"Obviously you've spent some time with her. I'm curious to hear what you've learned about her."

"She's a landscape architect. Used the money from the trust Buck set up for her to pay for her education. She came to Tanner's Crossing to return the money

and find her real father.'' He lifted a shoulder.
''That's about it. She doesn't talk much.''

''What about her as a person? What's she like?''

''She's a pro when it comes to landscaping. No
doubt about that. As to her personality, she's tough,
determined, independent. Wouldn't hesitate to call a
spade a spade. And she's defensive.'' He chuckled.
''Reminds me of a turtle. Walks around with her
shoulders up to her ears, as if she's expecting someone to throw her a punch.'' His smile melted as he
remembered the haunted look he'd seen in her eyes
the night before. ''Yet there's something about her
that's kinda sad,'' he said hesitantly.

''In what way?'' Maggie asked.

''I don't know,'' he said, unable to name the emotion he'd seen in her eyes. ''Like she's lost or something.''

''More than likely, she's suffering an identity crisis,'' Elizabeth interjected, then went on to explain to
the others at the table. ''Humans, by nature, draw
their identity from their parents. The death of her
mother and the discovery that the man she thought
was her father really wasn't her father has robbed her
of that identity. She's probably questioning who she
is right now, which would explain the lost look Rory
mentioned.

''It might explain her defensiveness, as well,'' she
went on. ''Knowing who you are and where you came
from gives a person a certain confidence. A sense of
security, if you will. I would imagine Macy's confidence has suffered a terrible blow, due to the loss of
her identity. I would imagine, too, that discovering
the lie has made her distrustful of everyone. After all,

if you can't trust your own mother, who can you trust?

"I may be wrong," she continued. "But if I were to offer an opinion, I'd say Macy's running scared right now, searching for an identity, something on which to base who she is. Until she does, it's likely that she feels trapped in what must feel like purgatory to her. She can't go backward. Her past, as she knew it, no longer exists. And she can't move forward, because the future seems out of reach for her. Until she's able to establish who her father is, who *she* is, she'll remain in a state of limbo."

Macy's trailer was small, designed more for weekend trips than as a permanent residence. Parked beneath a cottonwood tree, it lay in the shadows created by the umbrella of limbs overhead. Beyond the apron of shade, a lounge chair was positioned on a narrow strip of lawn to catch the last of the sun's rays. Macy lay on the chair, her feet bare, sunglasses shielding her eyes. Cutoffs revealed an amazing length of tanned leg, and a sawed-off tank top exposed a tempting band of flesh across her abdomen. Rory assumed that she was either asleep or dead, as she seemed unaware that he was parked on the street, watching her. Unlike her neighbors, he thought, with a glance over his shoulder at the couple who sat in lawn chairs across the street, eyeing him suspiciously.

With a sigh, he turned his gaze back to Macy, trying to work up the nerve to approach her. When he'd left the ranch, he hadn't planned to drop by for a visit, but throughout the drive to town, he hadn't been able to shake free of Elizabeth's theory of Macy suffering an identity crisis. He didn't have his sister-in-law's knowledge of psychology, but he had to admit, what she'd said made sense.

He supposed, if he was into psychoanalysis, the travel trailer Macy chose to live in supported Elizabeth's theory. The trailer was untethered, lacking permanence and stability, much like Macy's life at the moment. And it lacked an identity, a personality, as its exterior was painted beige, its only distinguishing mark a bold maroon stripe that ran down either side.

And that's what had drawn him here. Not Macy's trailer, but the woman who lived inside. He wanted to get to know Macy. Find out if Elizabeth's theory was right. Determine if Macy's porcupine demeanor was a defense mechanism, a sign of her loss of trust. To discover if she really did suffer an identity crisis, as a result of her mother's death and deception.

And he'd better start now, he thought, with another glance over his shoulder at her neighbors. If he remained in his truck much longer, those two busybodies across the street would probably call the cops and report him as a Peeping Tom. Anxious to avoid that unpleasantry, he climbed down from his truck and crossed to stand at the foot of the lounge chair…and discovered that the band of bare flesh at her waist was even more tempting up close.

"Working on your tan?" he asked.

She jumped at the sound of his voice, nearly overturning the lounge chair, then sat up and snatched off her glasses to glare at him.

"What are you trying to do?" she snapped. "Scare me to death?"

He hid a smile, thinking she was kind of cute when

she was mad. "No, but it looks like I did a good job of it."

Her frown deepening, she swung her legs over the side of the chair, dropped her elbows to her knees and buried her face in her hands. "I was asleep," she grumbled.

He slipped a finger beneath the thin strap of her tank top and swallowed a smile, when he felt a shiver move through her. "Cute pajamas."

She looked up at him, her eyes narrowed to slits. "Move it or lose it."

He slowly released the strap and lifted his hands. "I was just admiring your outfit."

She yanked the strap back into place. "What do you want?"

He lifted a brow. "A man has to have a reason to make a social call on a pretty lady?"

She huffed a breath and stood. "You can save the BS. I'm immune to men like you."

He gave the front of her top a pointed look. "I wouldn't be so sure."

She looked down, then quickly folded her arms across her chest to hide the embossed impressions her knotted nipples made on the thin fabric.

"I repeat," she said tersely. "What do you want?"

He lifted a shoulder. "I was on my way to the store and thought you might want to ride along. To check on the plants," he added, thinking that might be the inducement needed to persuade her.

She frowned at him a moment longer, then scooped her sandals from the ground and pushed past him. "Why not? I don't have anything better to do."

He stared after her, stunned that she'd agreed so easily. "You're actually going to go with me?"

She stopped and turned. "Have you watered the plants today?"

"No."

She turned for his truck again. "Then, yeah. I'm going. Somebody's gotta keep them alive."

Four

———

Macy squatted down to poke a finger into the mulch surrounding a red yucca, checking the soil for moisture. "Still damp," she confirmed. Standing, she dusted off her hands and looked around at the neighboring plants. "You're probably going to have to install a sprinkler system, though. This soil doesn't seem to retain much water."

"The woman is an idiot!"

Startled, Macy turned. "What woman?"

Rory flung out an arm, indicating the display window. "That damn window designer. She used stiffs. Stiffs! And after I specifically told her not to."

Stiffs? she thought in confusion as she stared at the display. "Are you talking about the mannequins?"

"Damn right I am! And that fence," he said, his face flushed with anger. "Does that look like the corner of a corral to you?"

Hesitant to comment one way or the other, she said, "Is it supposed to?"

"Hell, yes! White posts and rails," he muttered darkly. "That's the kind of fence you'd find in your Aunt Pitty-Pat's rose garden, not on a ranch. And get a load of that sand," he said, pointing to the floor of the display window. "Does that look like the kind of dirt you'd find in a corral? Hell, no!" he shouted before she could answer. "Throw in a couple of sand pails and you'd have yourself a damn beach."

She had to agree. The display was almost comical, what with the Aunt Pitty-Pat fence, the sand and the "stiffs" dressed up in western attire. "It's not that bad," she said, trying for diplomacy.

He looked at her as if she'd lost her mind. "Are you kidding me? Any cowboy worth his salt is going to laugh his head off when he sees this."

She lifted a shoulder. "If you're not satisfied, make her redo it."

"I can't! She's already gone! It would take days to get her back here again, and my grand opening is set for Wednesday."

"Well, why don't you redo it?" she said in frustration. "You obviously know what you want it to look like."

"Why do you think I hired a window designer in the first place? It takes artistic talent to dress a window, and although God was generous with me in most areas, he shorted me in that one."

He turned to look at the window again, his expression that of a little boy who'd dropped his ice cream cone without ever getting the first lick. "And I wanted this to be special," he said miserably. "This is my hometown. The place where I was born and raised. I wanted to give the folks here bragging rights as having the best darn western store in the state. I've invited the media and dignitaries from all over Texas to take part in the ribbon-cutting.

"I can just see the pictures in the newspapers now. The governor standing before this window, cutting the ribbon to signify the opening of Tanner's Cowboy Outfitters." He shook his head with regret. "Instead of giving the folks something to brag about, I'll have made Tanner's Crossing a laughingstock."

"Surely it isn't that bad," she said doubtfully.

He heaved a long-suffering sigh. "No. It's worse. Farmers. Ranchers. Cowboys. Those are the people who live around here and who'll do their shopping in my store. Country folks are prideful people who make their living with their hands and by the sweat of their brow." He gestured at the window. "That is an insult to them. It's a spoof of who they are, what they do, what they stand for."

As Macy stared at the window, she began to understand his concern. "Isn't there something you can do?"

"Nothing but tear the mess down. It'll leave me with an empty window, but I won't shame the folks here by letting it stay there."

That he would sacrifice what looked to be an expensive display for the sake of the townspeople stunned Macy. It also made her wonder if there wasn't more to Rory than she'd first thought.

She thrust out her hand. "Give me your keys."

Frowning, he dug a hand in his pocket to retrieve them. "Why?"

"We're going to fix this display and give the people of Tanner's Crossing the bragging rights they deserve."

It took less than an hour to strip the window of its contents, with Rory muttering threats all the while toward the woman he'd paid to design it. It took another hour and a half to drive out to the ranch, gather the supplies they needed and return to the store. By the time they'd moved everything inside and were ready to start on the window, the sun had set and a bar of track lighting was all that lit the interior of the display window. The heat from the lights turned the area into an oven.

Rory shoveled dirt from a wheelbarrow he'd wheeled in from outside, while Macy hammered a fence post onto a base.

"You're sure your family isn't going to mind that we took this stuff?" she asked for at least the third time.

He backhanded the sweat from his forehead, then scooped up another shovelful of dirt. "As I've told you at least three times already, what we took from the barn was nothing but junk."

She picked up another nail and positioned it on the base. "But what if they had planned to use it for something? They're going to be ticked when they go to get it and find it gone."

"They don't need it," he assured her.

"But what if they do?" she persisted.

He propped the shovel on the floor and rested his chin on top of the handle. "Has anybody ever told you that you're a worrywart?"

She looked up at him, then back down, frowning as she hammered the nail in place. "I'm not a worrywart. I merely have a conscience." She weathered him a look as she reached for another nail. "But I doubt you'd know what that is."

Hot and looking for an excuse to take a break, Rory set the shovel aside. "What makes you think I don't have a conscience?"

"Men like you seldom do."

He hunkered down beside her and drifted his fingers over the pile of nails, scattering them. "And what kind of man would that be?"

"A flirt."

"Sorry, but I don't see the connection."

"A flirt will tell a woman anything in order to seduce her, even if it's a lie. That indicates a lack of conscience."

He drew his chin back to look at her. "I beg your pardon, but I don't have to use flattery to seduce a woman."

Giving him a doubtful look, she pushed to her feet and lifted the pole, testing the strength of the base. "What do you think? Does this look sturdy enough?"

He stood and wiggled the post. "Looks good to me. And I don't use flattery to seduce women," he said again.

She picked up a weathered board and placed it against the post, eyeing it critically before setting it aside. "What method do you use?"

He trailed behind her as she picked up boards and aligned them, laying out a pattern to form the sides of the corral. "You make it sound premeditated," he complained. "When I make love to a woman, I don't plan it out beforehand. It just happens."

"Yeah, right," she muttered.

"Dammit, it does! There's something chemical, electric that happens between two people. When things are right between them, something clicks. You can't force it. It's either there, or it isn't."

"Do you want to make love to me?"

She'd asked the question as casually as she would ask the time. "Well, n-no," he stammered.

"Why not?"

He dragged a hand over the back of his neck, suddenly uncomfortable. "I don't know. Probably because you're not my type."

"And what's your type?"

"I like my women soft and feminine."

She glanced his way. "And I'm not?"

He knew he was walking on dangerous ground. If he wasn't careful, there was a strong chance he was going to hurt her feelings. "It's not that you're unattractive," he hedged. "It's just that...well, I like women with a little more—" he cupped his hands on his chest to demonstrate "—up front."

She turned to face him. "So you're saying that you wouldn't make love to me, that the *click* you mentioned wouldn't occur, because I have small breasts?"

"Well, yeah. I'd say that about sums it up."

She took a step toward him.

He choked a laugh and pushed out a hand. "Hey, now. What do you think you're doing?"

She lifted her hands and placed them on his shoulders. "Proving a point."

Something had changed in her expression, in her

eyes. Her features had softened, her eyes had turned molten. He watched in stunned silence as she swept her tongue over her lips, wetting them. His own mouth went dry as he stared at the gleaming results. She took another step that brought her body up flush against his. She was close. So close he could feel her heartbeat, as if it were his own, count the dark flecks that shimmered in her eyes. With her mouth now only inches from his, she stretched upward and pressed her lips to his.

Heat. That was his first thought. But it had barely registered before she opened her mouth over his and he was hit with the second thought. Need. It lashed through him like a whip, his knees buckling and his back bowing at the blow. Thanking the Good Lord that she wasn't his half sister, as she'd once thought, with a groan, he gripped her waist and hauled her up higher. With an urgency that sent his pulse racing, she knotted her fingers in his hair, thrust her tongue into his mouth, swept it over his teeth, nipped at his lips.

The heat raged higher, burning behind his eyes, scalding his throat. His only thought now was *where*. Where could he take her to make love to her? Not here in front of the window, where anyone who drove by could see them. The office? No. Nothing flat there but his desk, and it was covered with paperwork. The dressing rooms! They had benches. One of 'em would probably work as a makeshift bed.

He let her body slide slowly down his until her feet touched the floor. "The dressing room," he said against her mouth, and prayed they'd make it that far.

She dragged her lips from his with a reluctant slowness that churned need into desperation.

"That's not necessary," she whispered, her breath blowing warm against his chin. "I think I proved my point."

It took a moment for what she'd said to sink in. When it did, he flipped open his eyes to find her watching him, her lips pursed in a smug smile.

He yanked his hands from her waist, furious with himself for falling into her trap. "You didn't prove a thing."

"Oh, I think I did." Hiding a smile, she turned and headed for the door. "We'll finish this tomorrow," she called over her shoulder, then stopped and looked back at him. "The display, that is," she clarified, then walked out the door, laughing like a loon.

When Rory arrived at the store the next morning, he found Macy, looking all pink-cheeked and rested, watering his plants. And that irritated the hell out of him. How could she look so *normal* when his own system was tied up in knots and had been since she'd plastered that kiss on him?

Spotting him, she waved and called a cheery "Good morning!"

He curled his lip in a snarl. "I don't see what's so good about it."

She lifted a hand to the sky. "A clear, blue sky. Lots of sunshine. What more could a person ask for?"

"You out of my hair."

She made a tsking sound. "Don't tell me you're still upset about that kiss."

He braced his hands on his hips. "*Kiss?* Is that

what you call that liplocker you plastered on me last night?'' He advanced on her, murder in his eyes and on his mind. ''Well, I've got news for you, lady. Around here, we call that foreplay, and in case you're unfamiliar with the term, it's the one used to describe the sensual stimulation that leads to sex.''

Her face reddening, she quickly looked away. He knew he was making her uncomfortable, but he wasn't about to back off now. Not when he'd spent a very uncomfortable night himself, thanks to her.

''And I'm not talking about the missionary kind of sex,'' he continued, enjoying watching her squirm. ''I'm talking about the get-down-and-dirty-hot-and-sweaty kind of sex. The roll-around-on-the-floor-no-holds-barred kind of sex.

''Not that I'm opposed to a friendly kiss every now and again, you understand. But the kiss you laid on me was baited with promises of all kinds of carnal pleasure to come, then you up and walked away, without delivering on those promises. *That* kind of teasing would tick any man off.''

She set her jaw and aimed the hose at a group of crepe myrtles. ''My purpose in kissing you wasn't to turn you on. It was to prove a point. Which I did,'' she added stubbornly.

''Point?'' He scratched his head, as if confused. ''You're gonna have to refresh my memory. Exactly what point was it you were trying to make?''

''You said that you wouldn't make love to me because the stupid *click* you said was necessary between two people wouldn't occur because I have small boobs. *I* proved that it would.''

He held up a finger, as if remembering. ''Ah, yes.

The click. I do recall mentioning that. But as to you proving anything…'' He folded his arms over his chest and looked down his nose at her. ''You didn't prove a damn thing.''

Her jaw dropped. ''I most certainly did!''

''No,'' he argued pleasantly. ''To have proved anything, we would've had to make love, and as I recall, that didn't happen.''

''But you wanted to,'' she accused furiously.

''What I *want* to do and what I *do* do are two totally different things. And until we *do* make love, you haven't proved anything, except that you're a tease.''

Touching a finger to the brim of his hat, he walked away, confident that he'd succeeded in ruining what she'd claimed was a beautiful day.

Rory assigned Jimmy, a part-time high school student, to help Macy finish the display window. It wasn't that he wasn't willing to work alongside her to finish the job they'd started. He just had more important things to do. With his store's grand opening just two short days away, he had calls to make, arrangements to confirm and inventory to check, which is how he spent the bulk of his day.

It was after five when he heard a knock at his office door.

Thinking his manager had forgotten to tell him something before leaving, he called, ''Come on in.''

''Do you intend to uphold your end of our bargain?''

He glanced up to find a sullen-faced Macy standing in the doorway. Pleased to see that she hadn't recovered the cheerful mood she'd flaunted in his face that morning, he reared back in his chair and laced his fingers over his chest. "And what bargain would that be?" he asked, although he knew perfectly well what she was referring to.

"You agreed to help me find my father."

"That I did." He sat up and snagged a slip of paper from the top of his desk and held it out to her. "Sheila Tompkins married Ted Sawyer and now resides in Burnet, Texas."

She snatched the paper from his hand, scanned it, then glanced up at him, her eyes narrowed in suspicion. "How do you know for sure that this is the right Sheila?"

"Maw Parker. She's the undisputed town gossip. If you want to know anything, just ask Maw."

"Did you ask her about my mother?"

"I did. She remembered her but knew nothing about a pregnancy."

Grimacing, she stuffed the slip of paper into the back pocket of her overalls. "Jimmy and I finished the window display," she muttered. "You might want to take a look before I leave to make sure it's what you want."

He pushed back his chair and rose. "Good idea," he said, and followed her out.

She led him to the parking lot out front, then lifted a hand, indicating the window.

He stared, unable to believe the transformation. "Damn," he breathed. "It's better than I'd even imagined."

"So you're satisfied?"

"Satisfied?" He hooted a laugh, then slapped her

on the back. "I'm ecstatic! This is perfect. Absolutely perfect, right down to the cactus plant there in the corner." He moved in closer to study the details. "Is that real grass?" he asked, pointing.

"Yeah. Native. All the plants are real. Somebody's going to have to see that they get watered when they need it. I left instructions for their care with Jimmy."

He glanced at her over his shoulder. "Where did you get all this stuff?"

She lifted a shoulder. "Here and there."

He reached for his wallet. "How much do I owe you?"

Pushing out a hand, she turned away. "We're even."

"Even?" he called after her. "How can we be even?"

She patted her back pocket but kept walking. "You gave me the lead I needed."

After leaving the store, Rory drove out to the ranch to check on his house, telling himself he wasn't going to feel guilty about abandoning Macy. Sure, he'd left her to finish the window display alone that day, but he refused to feel guilty about that, since she'd volunteered for the job. And he hadn't welshed on their bargain to help her find her father, as his conscience kept insisting he had. Macy herself had said that he'd upheld his end when he'd come up with Sheila Tompkins's address.

But in spite of all his rationalizing, he couldn't stop his mind from creating a scorecard, listing what all she'd done for him in one column and what he'd done for her in the other. His side had two entries: the visit with Dixie he'd suggested and the call he'd made to Maw Parker that had resulted in the lead on Sheila Tompkins. Macy's side had two entries, as well: the landscaping for his store and decorating his display window.

Although the entries on the scorecard were even at two each, it didn't take a genius to figure out that the scales were weighted heavily in Macy's favor.

But she'd called them even, he told himself, and forced his mind to focus on what all the carpenters had done that day.

They'd started on the drywall, he noted as he walked through the house. The kitchen and bathroom cabinets installed; the electrical roughed in; the trim work complete. Another couple of weeks, a month at the outside, and his new home would be complete. Five thousand square feet of living space under one roof and another twelve hundred in porches and patios. More space than all of the apartments he currently leased added together—and more than a single man required. Hell, his new home was so big, he could probably fit ten travel trailers the size of Macy's inside.

Groaning, he did an abrupt aboutface. Macy again, he thought.

As he made his way back to the front of the house, his footsteps echoed hollowly in the empty rooms. The sound was a lonely one. Downright eerie, if he allowed himself to think about it. He snorted a laugh, remembering his fear of being alone when he was a kid. His brothers had given him grief over it. Even created a few situations, making him think he was alone, then laughing at his fear. But those days were long gone. Rory wasn't afraid of being alone any longer. He supposed he had his brothers to thank for curing him of the phobia. Humiliation was one hell of a tonic.

Stopping in the den, he braced a hand against the window and looked out, his heart warming at the western view of the ranch it provided. Stretched out before him, cattle grazed contentedly on pastures of thick green grass. Beyond them, miles of fencing stretched up into low hills covered with cedar and brush, a haven for a host of wildlife. At the moment, the sun sat atop the low hills, looking as if it had snagged there, painting the horizon in muted bands of red, gold and yellow, in its slow journey to sunset.

It felt good to be home again, he thought. It felt good to *have* a home. He had five apartments—one in each of the cities where he owned western stores—but not a one of them had ever felt like home. To him, they were merely places to sleep. Storage facilities for all of his belongings. But *this,* he thought, looking out at the spectacular view, this was home. The place where he'd grown up. The place where he planned to live out his life. Raise his family. With his brothers all living nearby now, his children and theirs would grow up playing together on the Bar-T, building memories together, just as he and his brothers had done.

He frowned, wondering what kind of memories Macy had to reflect on. With no siblings, her memories would certainly be different from his. In his estimation, growing up as an only child had to be hell. No built-in playmates. Nobody to give you grief when you did something stupid, or a slap on the back when you did something good. Nobody to tease you out of your fears. Nobody to talk to when you were lonely or just needed an ear. So who did she talk to when she ·wanted to unload? he wondered. With no siblings and her mother and stepfather both deceased, she had no family to turn to, no one to share her troubles with.

But, if the lead he'd given her paid off, she might be on her way to finding her father, which would give her a family again—or it would if the man was still alive and if he chose to establish a relationship with her. But those were mighty big "ifs." If even one of 'em didn't work out in her favor, then Macy would be right back where she started. Alone.

He remembered well her emotional state after they'd talked to Dixie. Though she'd tried her damnedest not to let him know how upsetting the meeting had been for her, she'd broken down before she could get inside her Jeep. He rubbed a hand over his chest, remembering the feel of her tears soaking through his shirt. The heat in them. The heartbreak. If her meeting with Sheila went the same as the one with Dixie, who would hold her this time? She was probably, right now, sitting all alone in that match-box-size trailer, crying her heart out and nobody there to mop up the mess.

He balled his fist against the window frame. He should've stuck with her, he told himself angrily. He should've honored the agreement he'd made with her. He'd told her he'd help her find her father and that meant sticking by her until the man was found, not providing her with a name and address and sending her off alone to search the guy out.

And knowing Macy, she hadn't wasted any time

starting the search. She'd probably taken the information he'd given her and hightailed it to Burnet to pay Sheila Tompkins a visit, which was a huge mistake in his estimation. When you wanted information from a person, you didn't go barreling in and demand it, which was exactly what he figured Macy would do. The woman was impatient, stubborn and about as subtle as a bulldozer.

Finesse. That's what was needed in a situation like this and finesse was Rory's specialty. Firming his lips, he turned for the door. He was going to help her he told himself as he locked up his house. She'd probably tell him to get lost, that she didn't want or need his help, just like the first time he'd offered it.

But if she did, that was too damn bad. The woman had no family. No one to turn to. She was alone in the world.

And Rory knew what it was like to be alone. The fear that could grab ahold of a person. His brothers might have cured him of his phobia, but he hadn't forgotten the feelings associated with it.

And nobody should have to suffer that kind of fear alone.

Macy sat with her hands pressed between her knees, trying to hide her impatience as she waited for Sheila's response.

"Pregnant?" Sheila repeated, her shock obvious. "Heavens. I had no idea. Darla Jean never said a word to me about being pregnant. All she told me before she left was that she was putting Tanner's Crossing behind her and was going to find herself a rich man to marry."

Macy tried her best to hide her disappointment. "She did get married. As to the rich part..." She lifted a hand. "I suppose she accomplished that, too. My stepfather had plenty of money, though he was pretty tight-fisted with it."

Sheila hooted a laugh. "Oh, I'll bet that made Darla Jean madder than a hornet. She expected a man to spend lavishly on her and had no patience for one that wouldn't."

Macy didn't need Sheila to tell her what Darla Jean was like. She'd experienced her mother's particular brand of selfishness firsthand. What she didn't know was who her father was.

Hoping to spur a memory that Sheila had forgotten, she asked, "Was there any one man in particular that my mother spent time with?"

Her face softening in sympathy, Sheila leaned to lay a hand on Macy's knee. "Oh, honey. I know you're wanting me to tell you who your father was, but I honestly don't know. Darla Jean liked all the men, and they liked her. I never knew her to spend any more time with one than any other."

Forcing a polite smile, Macy nodded, then stood. "Well, I guess I better be going. I've taken up enough of your time. Thanks for agreeing to talk to me."

Sheila wrapped an arm around Macy's shoulders and walked with her to the door. "Honey, I was glad to. I'm just sorry that I wasn't more help. I doubt anyone knows the answer. When Darla Jean left, she cut all her ties to Tanner's Crossing, including her one with me."

At the door, Macy paused. "If you should think of anything," she began.

Sheila gave her a sympathetic look. "I've got your number if I do."

With a nod, Macy turned to go. She was about to pull away from the curb when the screen door of Sheila's house flew open and Sheila came flying down the steps.

"Macy, wait!" she called, frantically waving a hand over her head.

Macy shoved the gearshift into Park and rolled down her window, praying that Sheila had remembered something. "Yes?" she asked expectantly.

Out of breath, Sheila thrust a small tin through the open window. "These are pictures of your mother and me and the crowd we ran with back then. I don't know what good they'll do you, but I'd thought you'd like to have them."

Her heart sinking, Macy accepted the tin. "Thanks. I'll make copies and return the originals to you."

Shaking her head, Sheila stepped back onto the curb. "No, you keep them. My husband never liked me having them around, anyway."

Five

The tin sat beside Macy's purse on the passenger seat as she made the drive back to Tanner's Crossing, but she refused to stop and open it, wanting the privacy of her trailer before she looked inside. Not that she expected to discover her father's identity hidden within. The tin held only pictures of her mother's past, a pictorial display Macy wasn't at all sure she wanted to see.

As she drove into Tanner's Crossing, instead of taking the loop that circumvented the downtown area, she turned onto the street that wound around the square and past Rory's store. She told herself she hadn't chosen the route in the hope of finding Rory there. She was merely checking on the landscape job she'd done, a follow-up she did after all her installations.

She slowed as she approached the corner and looked over the plants, pleased to see that they were thriving. But then her gaze slipped to the parking lot in front of the store. Disappointment sagged through her when she found it empty.

It's just as well, she told herself, and drove on. Even if Rory had been there she wouldn't have had the nerve to stop. He'd made it clear that he didn't want anything more to do with her and she certainly wasn't going to force herself on him. Not after what he'd said to her that morning.

A tease, she thought with a frown, remembering the name he'd called her. She wasn't a tease. That was more Darla Jean's style than Macy's.

But even if Macy were a tease, seduction was the furthest thing from her mind when she'd kissed him. She'd kissed him to prove a point. He'd insulted her, made her angry with his comment that she wasn't his type, that he liked his women softer, more feminine.

With bigger boobs.

Like she needed anyone to tell her she didn't have a figure that men drooled over. She had a mirror, didn't she? And even if she'd been born with the proper equipment, she never would've flaunted it. Throughout her life she'd watched her mother bat her eyes and show a little cleavage in order to get what she wanted from a man and Macy refused to lower herself to that form of persuasion. Using beauty and feminine wiles came with a price, indebting a woman to a man, leaving her weak, dependent and vulnerable to his every whim. And Macy didn't intend to get caught in the trap that had ensnared her mother. She had brains and initiative, and those two traits were the ones she'd used to get where she was and would continue to use throughout her life. Forget the helpless-buxom-blond persona her mother had perfected over the years. Even if Macy had been built for the role, she'd never have played it.

But just because she didn't approve of seduction as a form of barter didn't mean she was averse to men. Or kissing. Or sex, for that matter. Boobs or not, she was still a woman and had the same desires as one blessed with "more up front," as Rory had so vividly described her shortage.

And she'd never been more keenly aware of those desires than when Rory had responded to her kiss.

She blew out a breath, her blood heating at the mere memory. The man could kiss, she couldn't argue that. And he had moves that made every other man Macy had been with look like amateurs in comparison. Strong, clever hands; a rock-hard body; a face that would make a sculptor weep. And a smile that had the power to strip away even the strongest convictions. In retrospect, she could almost understand why her mother had attempted to trick Buck into marrying her. If the father was anything like his son, he would've been a hard man to resist.

Which was reason enough to steer clear of Rory, she told herself as she made the turn into the trailer park. From what she'd heard about Buck Tanner, he was a womanizer, lacking even an ounce of integrity. Definitely a person Macy would never want to become involved with.

So why did she still have this irrepressible desire to see Rory? Talk to him? Why did she wish he would—

Her thoughts scattered like leaves in the wind at the sight of Rory's truck parked on the street in front of her trailer. What was he doing here? she thought, panicking. She parked her Jeep in the allotted space in front of her trailer and tucked the tin inside her purse, stalling while she gathered her willpower like a shield around her.

By the time she climbed from her Jeep, he was walking toward her, his gait long and lazy, his hands stuffed into his pockets. Dressed in worn jeans and a chambray shirt the same shade of blue as his eyes, he looked good enough to eat, which wasn't at all fair, considering she'd already decided he was poison.

Shoving her purse strap over her shoulder, she eyed him suspiciously. "What are you doing here?"

He shrugged. "Thought I'd check on you. See if you went to Burnet."

Reminded of her visit with Sheila and the tin she'd slipped into her purse, she hugged her purse closer to her side. "I did."

He ducked his head to hide a smile. "Figured you wouldn't waste any time."

"I didn't see any point in waiting."

He glanced up and a shiver chased down her spine as his gaze met hers. The amusement was gone from his eyes and there remained only a soft warmth that looked dangerously like compassion.

"Want to tell me about it?"

"Not particularly."

"Have you eaten?"

Knocked off balance by the unexpected question, she shook her head. "No."

"Wanna grab some takeout and drive out to the ranch with me? You can see the house I'm building."

Good sense told her to refuse. Hadn't she less than

five minutes before convinced herself that he wasn't the kind of man she wanted to become involved with?

She released the breath she'd been holding.

"Yeah," she heard herself say. "Sounds good."

With a bucket of fried chicken and Macy as passengers, Rory drove down the path toward his house, bouncing his truck over rocks and swerving around holes deep enough to lose a tire in. He glanced over at Macy, who had her eyes riveted to the path ahead and a death grip on her seat.

"Sorry about the bumpy ride," he said, and slowed. "I'm waiting until the house is finished before putting in a road. Figure the construction trucks would tear one up if I were to put it in now."

She nodded. "Probably wise."

"We're not far," he assured her, then gestured up ahead. "If you look closely at that group of trees, you can see the top of the chimney."

She strained to look, her eyes rounding as the house came into sight. "Oh, my gosh," she murmured. "It's beautiful."

Pleased that she'd think so, he parked as close to the house as he could and grabbed the bucket of chicken. "Come on inside and I'll show you around."

He waited for her at the hood of the truck, then led the way. "Watch where you step," he warned, dodging a pile of discarded lumber. "No telling what you might step on."

He heard a grunt and glanced back to find Macy straining to drag a sheet of discarded plywood off what looked to him to be scrub brush.

"What are you doing?" he asked in dismay.

Her teeth bared, she strained to move the sheet of wood. "Trying to save this shrub."

Grimacing, he retraced his steps. "Cleanliness isn't one of the men's strong points, that's for sure. There's a Dumpster for them to use, but they rarely do."

Before he could take it from her, she shoved the plywood away and dropped to her knees to examine the flattened bush.

"Oh, you poor thing," she moaned as she tried to straighten its bent limbs.

He caught her hand and pulled her to her feet. "Don't worry. Once the house is finished, I'm planning to hire a landscaper to put everything back in order."

"By then it'll be too late," she said miserably, dragging her feet behind him.

Frowning, he unlocked the door, then stood back, letting her enter before him. "You think so?"

"If the necessary precautions aren't taken before and during the construction process, the root systems of surrounding trees are damaged and all the natural vegetation destroyed."

He handed her the bucket of chicken, upended two empty five-gallon paint buckets, then motioned for her to sit while he sat down opposite her. "Is there anything I can do now to keep that from happening?"

She lifted the lid from the bucket of chicken and peered inside. "Other than fire all the men currently working on the job?"

He gave her a wry look. "I can't do that. These guys may be slobs, but they're skilled craftsmen and good at what they do."

She plucked out a chicken leg and took a bite before passing the bucket to him. "Then you need to implement damage control. First, you clean up the mess that already exists. Second, you put the fear of God in the workers. Threaten to dock their pay every time one of them fails to use the Dumpster you've provided. Third, or sooner, if you can squeeze it in, hire a landscaper. Somebody with experience working around construction and who knows what protective measures to take. Somebody who wouldn't hesitate to rip the guys a new one if they're caught harming any of the plants.''

He lifted a brow. "Got anyone in mind?"

She glanced up at him, then rolled her eyes. "That wasn't a hint that you hire me."

He took a bite of his chicken and hid a smile as he chewed. "Didn't say it was. But you obviously have the knowledge and, from what I've seen, wouldn't hesitate to go nose to nose with anyone who didn't see things your way."

She pursed her lips. "I don't know whether I should be flattered or insulted."

Laughing, he tossed his chicken bone into a nearby trash can. "Flattered. The job is yours, if you want it."

She rose and crossed to the window, worrying her lower lip as she looked out, obviously tempted by the offer.

"It's a big job to take on," she murmured, as if thinking aloud. "I'd have to do a site survey. Develop a preliminary design. Inventory what plants can be saved. Remove those that are beyond help. Which means I'd need equipment." She glanced over her shoulder at him. "What I reserved from the sale of my business is in storage. I only have with me the tools that I bought to do the landscaping job for your store.''

''You can buy what you need and charge it to me. I've got accounts in every store in town.''

She stared at him a long moment, then turned back to look out the window. ''But what if I'm not around long enough to finish the job?''

''I'll take whatever time you have to give.''

Her gaze on the landscape beyond, she drew in a deep breath, then turned. ''I'll do it.''

He shot her a wink. ''I was hoping you would.''

She crossed back and selected another piece of chicken before sitting down again. ''I hope you're wanting to go with a natural landscape,'' she said. ''This setting is perfect for it, plus you've got the advantage of having all the existing vegetation to work with. That alone will save you a ton of money.''

''You're the boss. Whatever you think best.''

She took a bite and chewed, frowning thoughtfully. ''Of course, you'll want to enhance what's here. Create points of interest. Water features are always nice, but you've got to know going in that they aren't maintenance-free. And considering your location, you'll have to plan around whatever wildlife is present. Are deer a problem?''

He was having trouble following the conversation. She kept darting out her tongue to lick at a crumb caught in the corner of her mouth.

''Deer?'' he repeated dully.

''You do have deer on the ranch, don't you?'' She paused to lick at the stubborn crumb again. ''I'd think with all the raw land and woods, deer would consider this area a buffet.''

Totally transfixed by her mouth, he said vaguely, "Yeah. I guess."

"There are things you can do to keep them from feeding close to your house and destroying your landscape. Higher fencing is one option, but not one I'd necessarily recommend. If you enjoy watching the deer and want only to dissuade them from feeding near your house, you can plant things they don't like to eat."

Her voice faded to a drone as he found himself thinking about that kiss she'd plastered on him and the way her mouth had felt on his…the way she'd tasted…the way her body had moved sensuously against his…the heat the friction had stoked.

"Rory? Rory!"

He gave himself a shake. "What?"

"Are you okay?"

"Yeah. Fine. Why?"

She took a napkin from the sack, eyeing him suspiciously as she wiped her hands. "You had this… I don't know. *Look* on your face. Like you were contemplating your next meal and I was it."

Since that pretty much described what he'd been thinking—and was *still* thinking—he had to smile. "You do look mighty tasty."

Sputtering a laugh, she balled up her napkin and tossed it into the trash can. "I'd just as soon you stuck with the chicken, if you don't mind."

He dropped the piece he held back into the bucket, his appetite gone—at least, where food was concerned. "I sure do like your mouth."

Caught in the act of picking up her purse, she froze, then slowly straightened, leaving it where it lay. "Where did *that* come from?"

"It was what I was thinking."

She blew out a breath. "Well, think about something else."

He leaned forward, resting his elbows on his knees, and teased her with a smile. "Does knowing that I think about your mouth make you uncomfortable?"

She eased around on the bucket, as if preparing to run, if the need should arise. "Well…yeah. Wouldn't it make you uncomfortable?"

"Depends on who was doing the thinking. Now, if it was you—" standing, he pulled her to her feet and dropped his arms to loop them loosely at her waist "—I'd think that was just fine."

Since his face was bare inches from hers, there was little else Macy could do but think about his mouth. Full lower lip, the upper shaped with a well-defined bow at its center. One corner of his mouth seemed to curve naturally upward, as if he were amused at some private joke.

She closed her eyes and gulped, remembering the feel of his mouth on hers and wishing that if he was going to kiss her, he'd hurry up and do it. The anticipation, the expectancy was slowly killing her.

She felt the warmth of his breath against her face, the feather-light brush of his lips across hers before he settled at their center in a kiss that stole her breath. A low hum of satisfaction rumbled low in his throat and he tightened his arms around her waist, drawing her nearer, taking the kiss deeper.

Sensation after sensation rippled through her in waves. Mesmerized by them—by *him*—she swallowed back a low moan of disappointment when he withdrew.

"The sun will be setting soon," he said, and caught

her hand. "I've got a blanket in the truck. Let's go outside and watch."

Numb, she stumbled after him, unable to think of anything beyond the fact that he'd ended the kiss when she'd wanted it to go on and on.

At his truck, he tugged a blanket from the back seat and headed for a low hill in the distance. Once there, he released his hold on her to shake out the blanket, letting it drift to the ground like a cloud, then dropped down on it and offered her a hand.

"Come on," he urged. "You don't want to miss this."

Placing her hand in his, she folded her legs beneath her and sank down beside him, turning her face to the west, where the sun perched on the horizon like a ball of fire.

"Oh, wow," she murmured, awed by the sight. "That's really something."

Stretching out on his side, he propped himself up on an elbow and laid a hand on her knee. "It's that," he said with a sigh.

They sat in silence, watching as the sun made its slow descent, its rich colors bleeding into the sky. The only sounds to disturb the quiet were the whir of cicadas and an occasional low bawl from the herd of cattle grazing in a pasture nearby.

After a while, Macy became aware of the slow stroking of his fingers along her thigh. He wasn't aware of the movement, she was sure, yet it sent warmth flooding through her. She stole a glance his way and found him looking at her. Her heart skipped a beat at the softness she found in his gaze, the heat.

Reaching up, he tucked a strand of hair behind her ear. "I remember the first time I saw you I thought that your hair looked as if a sheep shearer had gotten ahold of you.''

Insulted, she tried to duck away, but he cupped a hand at the back of her neck and held her in place.

"But I have to say, the style is growing on me." He drew her down to lie beside him and leaned to bump his nose against hers. "*You're* growing on me.''

She stilled, her gaze freezing on his.

Biting back a smile, he dipped his head to nuzzle her neck, then drew back and frowned. "What perfume is that you're wearing? It has a floral scent but isn't sickly sweet like some I've smelled.''

"It's—" She cleared her throat and tried again. "It's not perfume. It's lavender water.''

"Never heard of it.''

"Specialty shops carry it, but I make my own.''

He shifted to lie on his side, using his arm as a pillow. "I always thought you were talented. You just proved me right.''

She sputtered a laugh. "Any fool can make lavender water.''

"You're the first woman I've ever known to do it. That makes you special. Unique.''

Embarrassed, she lifted a shoulder and let it drop. "That's something, I suppose.''

"You're filled with a whole lot of somethings.'' He caught her hand and lifted it to examine. "Take your hands, for instance. You know what I'm thinking when I look at them?''

She curled her fingers inward, trying to hide her chipped nails. "What? That they look like a field hand's?''

His gaze on hers, he drew her hand to his lips and

pressed a kiss against her knuckles. "No. I wonder what they would feel like on me."

Her breath caught in her throat.

Smiling, he dropped her hand to his chest and held it there. "Want to show me?"

"I—I don't think—"

He leaned in and brushed his mouth over hers. "Don't think. Thinking is reserved for things of the mind. What we're talking about here is purely physical."

She gulped, then slowly unfurled her fingers until her hand was splayed wide.

He covered it with his.

"Hot," he murmured. "Even with my shirt between us, your hand burns like a brand against my chest." He leaned to touch his mouth to hers and reached for the first button of his shirt. "Let's see what it feels like on my skin."

As he teased her lips with his, he freed each button in turn. When he reached the waist of his jeans, he tugged his shirttail free, then quickly unbuttoned the last three. She didn't wait for an invitation, but opened her hands over his chest. She heard his low moan of pleasure, felt its vibration against her lips as her flesh met his for the first time. Unable to resist, she pushed her hands upward, shoved his shirt over his shoulders, then dragged her palms back down.

He might've started this, Rory thought, but she had definitely taken over the reins. The kiss was hers now, her lips demanding as she forced his back to the blanket. Her hands seemed to be everywhere at once—in his hair, gliding over his chest, framing his face. Shifting over to straddle him, she took the kiss deeper.

He fitted his hands at her waist and allowed himself

a moment for shock. He'd never imagined that beneath that tomboy exterior lurked such a sexy woman. She was so…hot. So aggressive. But he didn't intend to waste any time mulling over the revelation. He intended to enjoy.

With that single goal in mind, he guided her legs down, fitting her body along the length of his, anxious to experience every facet of this irresistible and totally amazing side of her he'd discovered.

He roamed his hands down her back and proved what he'd already known. She was slim as a reed…but firm. There wasn't an ounce of fat anywhere on her. Not on her back. Not on her waist. Not on her thighs. Cupping his hands on the cheeks of her butt, he brought her up against him and swallowed a groan as she rocked her pelvis over his length. The woman might taste like sweetness and light, but her moves were pure sin.

Curiosity drew his hands upward beneath the hem of her blouse and to the clasp of her bra. Unhooking it, he smoothed his hands up her ribs until his palms rested on the soft swell of her breasts. He increased the pressure, heard her mewl of pleasure and slipped his hands between their bodies to cup them fully. Her breasts were small, as he'd guessed, but firm and round, her nipples distended buds of sensual pleasure.

Anxious to taste her, he sat up and flipped her to her back, then leaned to shove her blouse to her neck and expose her breasts. Shades lighter than the skin surrounding them, her breasts gleamed like fine porcelain in the fading sunlight, a temptation he couldn't have resisted even if he'd wanted to. He raked a thumb over one nipple, watched it darken as the blood rushed to it, then opened his mouth over it and drew her in.

She arched up at the first contact, her back bowing, then knotted her fingers in his hair and held him to her as he suckled.

He lifted his head. "Forget what I said about small breasts," he said. He squeezed a hand around the breast he'd suckled, shaping it within his palm, then dipped his head to lick the glistening nipple that protruded from its center. "I was wrong," he admitted, then closed his mouth over it again with a groan.

While he suckled, he toed off his boots and stripped off his jeans, then went to work on her slacks. Within seconds he was tossing them aside, along with her panties and easing down into the nest she'd created for him between her legs.

Dragging himself higher, he rained kisses over her face. "Do we need protection?"

She dug her fingers into his buttocks. "No. Just hurry."

He spread his lips across hers in a smile. "And ruin all the fun?"

"Rory—"

He liked hearing her say his name, felt a smug sense of pleasure at the impatience her tone held at the moment. But he didn't intend to rush this. Not when he had a whole night of pleasure to look forward to. Intending to take advantage of every second, he dragged his lips down her neck, nipping and teasing his way to her breasts. He suckled slowly, drawing pleasure from each drag of his lips and hopefully pleasing her in return.

He smoothed a hand over her belly and felt the shiver that shook her as he curved his fingers over her feminine mound. Though the urge to touch her there was strong, he resisted and moved on to stroke his hand down her thigh, then back up. Her legs parted instinctively, and this time he couldn't resist. He dipped his fingers into the juncture of her legs, found her center, the slick, moist heat.

"Rory, please…"

He couldn't ignore the desperation in her plea, wouldn't have even if he could, as the same desperation burned through him.

Shifting on top of her, he guided his sex to hers, then found her hands. Lacing his fingers through hers, he pushed her hands up to hold them against the blanket above her head and closed his mouth over hers. He rocked his hips against hers, pushing himself inside, then filled her mouth with a groan as pleasure knifed through him.

He held himself, unmoving, savoring the feel of her around him, giving her the time she needed to adjust to his size, his length. Passion built, as did the heat, and he thrust hard, burying himself deeply inside her. He felt the clamp of her feminine walls around him, the quiver of her legs beneath his and ground his hips against hers, giving her his full length, the satisfaction she demanded.

Arching high to meet him, she came apart in an explosion of heat that stole his breath. His body responded, his sex pulsing, his body jerking, as he emptied himself inside her.

Spent, he rolled on his back, taking her with him, and wrapped his arms around her. Weak, he slowly became aware of the butterfly stroke of her fingers along the side of his face, the warm moistness of her breath as she released it in a sigh against his chest.

Smiling, he curved a hand over the back of her head and pressed a kiss against her hair. "So tell me. What did you think of that sunset?"

Weaving her legs with his, she snuggled close. "What sunset?"

Though spending the night with Macy on a blanket spread beneath a canopy of stars had a certain appeal, the lack of amenities the outdoors offered forced Rory to suggest that they return to her trailer, where they spent the remainder of the night. The bed in her trailer was more a bunk than a bed and they had to arrange themselves spoonlike in order for them both to fit.

But Rory didn't mind the crowded quarters. Not when it meant he got to sleep with Macy's hot little body snugged up against his, his head resting on the pillow behind hers.

He was the first to wake the next morning, and he lay there a moment, enjoying the unexpected pleasure of finding himself in her bed. But a busy day lay ahead, one jam-packed with activities surrounding the grand opening of his store.

Knowing he couldn't laze around in her bed any longer, he tucked his nose in the tempting curve between her shoulder and neck. "Wake up, sunshine," he whispered, nuzzling. "Time to get moving."

She stretched like a cat, arching her back, her feet braced against his legs, then moaned and went limp.

"What time is it?" she murmured sleepily against the pillow.

He rolled his wrist to look at his watch. "Quarter after six."

She tugged the sheet to her chin and burrowed

deep. "Roosters don't even get up this early," she complained.

Laughing, he dropped a kiss on her bare shoulder. "This rooster does," he informed her as he climbed over her. "The grand opening is in two days and I've got a ton of work to do to prepare for it."

She shifted, moving into the spot he'd vacated, and yawned as she settled her head on the pillow again. "I'd offer to make you breakfast, but I'm not much of a cook."

He pushed his legs into his jeans, then pulled them up. "You're not even going to offer me a cup of coffee?"

Whimpering pitifully, she threw back the covers. "If I have to." She swung her legs over the side of the bed, then sat there a moment, scrubbing her hands over her face as if trying to wake up.

Rory stared, his request for coffee forgotten. Totally nude, she created a picture much more tempting than caffeine. He tossed aside the shirt he'd picked up, buried a knee in the mattress beside her hip and pushed her back. "Maybe later," he said as he stretched out over her. "Right now I've got a hankerin' for you."

Six

This was the problem with getting physical with a guy, Macy told herself as she dug a narrow trench around a tree beside Rory's house. If the sex was good, you couldn't get the guy off your mind. If it was bad, you didn't give the guy another thought. But if it was *really* good, it was worse, because then you started trying to think of ways to get more. Whereas, if it was *really* bad, it was merely an inconvenience. You had your phone number changed.

Sex with Rory had definitely been better than good, which was why she couldn't keep her mind focused on anything for longer than two seconds at a time before thoughts of him came drifting back in to distract her.

And distractions were not what she needed right now, she thought, as she stole a surreptitious glance at the painter who was exiting the house through the rear kitchen door. When she'd arrived that morning and gotten her first look at the workmen on the job, she'd known immediately that she was in for trouble. She'd worked with men like them before. Dumb, macho blockheads who thought a woman's place was in his bed.

She'd introduced herself, told them Rory had hired her as his landscaper and that she had his permission to fire any man on the spot who was caught littering or damaging any of the vegetation. It was stretching the truth a little but she figured in order to put the fear of God in them, she was going to have to use extreme measures, which, in her book, included lying.

Though she kept digging, pretending to be busy, she kept an eye on the painter, watching as he set paint pails filled with brushes on a crude table constructed from a couple of sawhorses and a sheet of cracked plywood. She knew what he was planning to do. He intended to clean his paintbrushes, then dump the mineral spirits he'd used to clean them with on the ground. She'd seen it done a zillion times. It was a quick, easy method of disposing unwanted chemicals but hell on the soil and vegetation that soaked it up.

Knowing she had to make a stand, let these men know she expected them to abide by her rules, she leaned her shovel against the tree and moved quietly to stand within six feet of the man. Just as he lifted the first pail to dump, she said, "I wouldn't do that if I were you."

He jumped, startled, then scowled and lifted the pail again. "And who's gonna stop me?"

She clamped a hand down on his arm. "I am."

He gave her a slow look up and down and snorted a breath. "Maybe you and a team of sumo wrestlers." He tried to shake off her hand. "Get outta my way. It's five o'clock and I'm thirsty for a beer."

"You know that I'll have to fire you if you dump that here," she warned.

He sneered. "I don't take no orders from no woman. Rory Tanner hired me. He'll be the one to fire me."

She gave him a tight smile. "Well, guess we'll have to see about that, won't we?" Before he knew what she intended, she hooked a foot behind his ankle and jerked, managing to snatch the paint pail from his hand before he sat down hard on his butt.

Addled, he gave his head a shake, looked up at her, then came up off the ground with a growl. He charged, his head ducked low, and caught her just above the knees with his shoulder and took her down, sending the pail's contents shooting into the air and down over both of them as they landed in a pile.

Pinned beneath him, she shoved at his shoulders. "You're fired. Do you hear me? Fired! Get your equipment and get off this job *now!*"

He lifted his head, his teeth bared, his eyes filled with hatred. "Ain't no woman gonna tell me what to do."

He clamped a wide hand over her throat, squeezed. Her eyes wide, her mouth open and moving soundlessly, Macy clawed at his hand. She knew she had to do something and quickly, but before she could think of a way to break free, the painter was hurtling backward through the air and Rory was kneeling over her, smoothing her hair back from her face.

"Macy, are you okay?"

Hearing the concern in his voice, the worry, she nodded, then struggled to sit up, holding a hand to her burning throat. "I—fired—him," she managed to choke out.

He glanced over his shoulder to where the painter lay moaning. His jaw hardened and he looked back at her. "If you hadn't, I would've." He gently took her by her arms and helped her to her feet. "You're sure you're okay?" he asked as he guided her toward his truck.

She rubbed at her throat, nodded. "Fine," she croaked.

He looked her up and down, as if needing to verify for himself that she hadn't received any other injuries, then boosted her up onto the passenger seat. When he was sure she was settled comfortably, he glanced back over his shoulder again. "I'll be right back," he said, then slammed the door.

Wide-eyed, Macy watched him stalk back over to the painter, who was standing but rocking unsteadily on his feet. Rory grabbed him by the front of his shirt, pulled back a fist and plowed it into the man's face. Blood spurted from his nose as the painter fell like a brick, knocked cold.

"Billy!" Rory yelled.

A man ran from inside the house, his face pale, obviously having witnessed the entire scene.

"Yes, sir?"

Rory flung out a hand, indicating the man on the ground. "Take Joe to the doctor and have him patched up. Tell 'em to send the bill to me. When you're done, I want you to get back here, pack up your gear and your crew and clear out. Nobody who would stand by and watch a woman harmed is going to work for me.''

Hanging his head in shame, Billy nodded.

Sitting on the kitchen table in Rory's apartment, planted there by Rory himself, Macy shoved impatiently at his hand. ''Would you stop it!'' she cried. ''I just got the wind knocked out of me for a minute. I'm okay now.''

Ignoring her, he continued to probe and prod. ''You could have suffered internal injuries. A broken rib. A punctured lung.'' Paling, he picked up her purse and shoved it into her hand. ''I'm taking you to the hospital.''

She tossed the purse away. ''I've already told you, I'm not going to the hospital.''

He plucked his cell phone from the clip on his belt. ''Then I'm calling Ry and have him come and check you over.''

She snatched the phone from his hand and tossed it on the table behind her. ''You're not calling anybody. It's bad enough that I have to put up with your prodding and poking. I'm not letting your brother get any cheap thrills by groping me, too.''

Flattening his lips, he hitched his hands on his hips and glared at her, then went limp as a rag and gathered her into his arms. ''God, Macy. He could have killed you.''

She gulped but refused to let him know how truly frightened she'd been. ''He wasn't going to kill me.

Another couple of minutes, and I'd have had him crying 'uncle.'"

He drew back to look at her. "Are you kidding me? Another couple of minutes and he'd have snapped your neck."

The blood drained from his face at the suggestion and she tugged him back to stand between her legs, afraid he was going to faint. "He didn't hurt me," she told him for what seemed the umpteenth time. "I'm fine. I promise." She held her arms out, so that he could get a good look at her. "See? There's nothing wrong with me."

He caught her arm and turned it over. "What's that?"

She looked down, then scowled and rubbed at the spot. "Paint. I was holding a bucket of paint when Joe tackled me."

He scooped her off the table, wrapping her legs around his waist. "Let's get you in the tub and get you cleaned up."

His concern touched her, but she couldn't let him continue to worry about her when there was nothing wrong with her. Locking her arms around his neck, she pushed her face up to his. "Is this a trick to get me naked?"

He stopped, stared, then continued on to the bathroom. "No, but now that you mention it, it sounds like a damn good idea."

At the side of the tub, he gently set her down on its edge, then leaned to turn on the water. After he'd satisfied himself with the temperature, he toed off his boots and dragged his T-shirt over his head.

As he reached for his belt buckle, she lifted a brow. "I thought I was the one who needed a bath?"

"You are," he assured her, then grinned and shoved his jeans down his legs. "But I figure it'll makes things a whole lot easier if I'm in the tub with you when I bathe you."

"Uh-huh," she hummed doubtfully.

He reached around her to nab a bottle of bath oil from a shelf. "Do you prefer a floral or herbal scent?" he asked as he examined the label.

"You keep a supply of bubble bath on hand?" she asked incredulously, then held up a hand. "Never mind. I don't want to know."

He poured a liberal dose over the water, stirred, then climbed into the tub and offered her his hand. "Easy," he warned as she stepped over. "I don't want you slipping and falling."

She rolled her eyes. "I'm not helpless."

"Indulge me." He sank down behind her, then guided her down into the water to sit between his legs. "Comfortable?" he asked.

Comfortable? she thought. Who could possibly be comfortable sitting in the bathtub between a naked man's legs? Especially if the naked man was Rory. "I'm fine," she lied.

Satisfied, he slipped his arms beneath hers and drew her back to lie against his chest, wrapping his arms around her middle and locking his ankles over her legs. "We'll soak for a minute before we get down to scrubbin'."

Lulled by the warmth of the water and the comfort of his body wrapped cocoonlike around hers, Macy closed her eyes. "Yeah. Whatever."

She dozed for a minute—it couldn't have been longer than that, she was sure—but roused when she felt his breath at her ear.

"Macy?" he said softly.

"Hmm?"

"Wake up, honey. The water's getting cold."

She stretched, then groaned, hugging her arm against her middle.

"What's wrong?" he asked, immediately concerned.

She rubbed at her sore muscle. "Nothing. Just sore. It's been a while since I wrestled with a man."

His lips curved against her hair in a smile. "Well, we'll have to see what we can do about that."

Holding her away from him, he stood, then stepped over the side of the tub and grabbed a towel. He dried off quickly, then nabbed a fresh towel and held it open for Macy, wrapping it around her as she stepped from the tub.

"Hang on," he said, turning away. "I'll see what I can find for you to put on."

When he returned he was wearing a pair of sweatpants and a T-shirt and offered Macy the same. "They'll probably swallow you whole," he said, "but they're clean."

Touched by his thoughtfulness, she quickly stepped into the pants and cinched the drawstring at her waist, then pulled the T-shirt over her head. Looking down, she read the phrase printed across its front and bit back a smile as she looked up at him. "Cowboys do it in the dirt?"

He hooked an arm around her waist and guided her

from the bathroom. "And anywhere else you can think of. Cowboys just like to do it."

At the door of his bedroom, Macy stopped, staring at the king-size bed. Covered with a leopard-print spread of crushed velvet and a mountain of sumptuous pillows, it screamed "bachelor pad." And all she could think about was how many women he'd shared the bed with.

Turning away, she pushed past him. "Do you mind taking me back to my house?" she asked, hoping he didn't hear the strain in her voice. "I'd really like to sleep in my own bed tonight."

He fell in behind her, cupping her elbow in his hand. "Sure, honey. Whatever you want."

She knew by his sympathetic tone that he thought her reasons for wanting the familiarity of her own bed had to do with the upsetting scene with Joe.

But that was fine with Macy. Let him think what he would. At least in her bed, she knew she wouldn't be haunted by ghosts of other women.

The parking lot and streets surrounding Rory's store were packed, forcing Macy to park three blocks away and make the long hike back for the private party Rory had planned to follow his opening. Pausing at the door, she shoved the thin spaghetti strap of her sundress back onto her shoulder. She rarely wore dresses and wouldn't be wearing one now if Rory hadn't insisted that she attend his party. She didn't know why he had invited her. Festivities like this were reserved for family and close friends and she was neither.

And it was the uncertainty of their relationship, her

inability to define it, that put the frown on her face as she opened the door to his western store.

One step inside, she stopped and stared, sure that the entire population of Tanner's Crossing had gathered to help him celebrate his grand opening. The clothing and display racks had been pushed back against the walls, creating space for a single, long row of buffet tables. People stood in loose groups at either side laughing, talking and eating, while waiters, decked out in western attire, wove their way through the room offering guests flutes of champagne.

Heat crawled up Macy's neck when she realized that her entrance had drawn several curious looks—a few from people she remembered approaching with questions about her mother when she'd first arrived in town. Feeling conspicuous and totally out of place, she decided to make a quick exit. But as she turned to leave, she heard her name called and glanced back to find a woman hurrying her way.

"I'm so glad you finally made it," the woman said, and grabbed her hand. "You probably don't remember me, but I'm Elizabeth Tanner, Rory's sister-in-law."

It took a moment for Macy to place the woman. "Yeah," she said slowly. "You're Woodrow's wife."

Smiling, Elizabeth drew her with her toward the party. "I promised Rory that I would keep an eye out for you. He was afraid you'd take one look at this wild crowd and turn tail and run."

Since that was exactly what she had planned to do, Macy remained silent.

"We were all surprised when Rory told us he'd invited you," Elizabeth continued.

Stunned, Macy jerked to a stop.

Laughing, Elizabeth patted her arm. "I didn't mean that we were surprised that he'd invited *you* particularly. It's just that Rory usually doesn't bring a date to these social functions." She leaned close to whisper, "He prefers to remain footloose and fancy free, if you know what I mean."

"Yeah," Macy said wryly. "I think I do."

Before Elizabeth could say more, another woman joined them. Maggie, if Macy remembered correctly. Ace's wife.

"Thank goodness you're here," Maggie said in relief. "I've had to all but hog-tie Rory to keep him from leaving and going after you. And he's the host, for heaven's sake! You'd think the man would know he can't leave his own party."

Macy stared, unsure what to say but Maggie saved her from a reply by grabbing her other hand.

"Come on," she urged, and gave her a tug. "Let's find him and tell him you're here, before he makes the social blunder of the year by leaving."

Trapped between Rory's sisters-in-law, Macy had no choice but go along with them. A glass of champagne was shoved into her hand at the same moment she spotted Rory. As if sensing her presence, he glanced her way. A smile spread across his face and he shot her a wink then quickly separated himself from the group of men he was talking to and headed her way.

"I see you found her," he said to his sisters-in-law.

"We did," Maggie confirmed, then frowned at the buffet table. "You're running low on champagne," she said, then gave his cheek a distracted pat and turned away, saying, "But don't worry. Elizabeth and I will take care of it."

Left alone with Rory, Macy was struck by a sudden attack of shyness. "Great party."

"It is now that you're here." He caught her hand and gave her an appreciative look up and down. "That sure is a pretty dress," he said, then drew her hand to his lips. "But personally, I prefer you in nothing at all."

Her cheeks blazing, she shot a furtive glance around. "Have you lost your mind?" she whispered furiously. "Someone might have heard you."

Laughing, he looped an arm around her waist and guided her toward the buffet table. "What's wrong? Afraid I'll ruin your reputation?"

She shot him a sour look. "No. I was more worried about me bolstering yours."

As the evening wore on, Macy actually found herself enjoying the party. Not that surprising, really, since Rory's family made every effort to see that she had a good time. Each time Rory was forced to leave her side, one or the other of his sisters-in-law would head her way and chat with her until he returned. His brothers did their part, too, by seeing that her champagne glass remained full. As a result of their attentiveness, by the time the guests were all gone and the caterers had cleared out, Macy was feeling a little tipsy.

She probably looked it, too, since Rory insisted upon driving her home.

While she waited for him to unlock her trailer door, she leaned her head against his shoulder and sighed wistfully. "Do you realize how lucky you are?"

He glanced her way then pulled open the door and placed a hand low on her back. "How's that?" he asked as he guided her inside.

She tossed her purse onto the sofa, then dropped down beside it, exhausted but content. "To have such a big family."

Loosening his tie, he sat down beside her and draped an arm along the sofa behind her. "It has its pluses."

"They're all so nice." She tipped her head back against his arm and smiled up at the ceiling. "Even Woodrow, which really surprised me, considering he's so big and intimidating."

Hiding a smile, he brushed a knuckle across her cheek. "Trust me. They're not always that nice. Tonight they were using their party manners."

"Party manners," she repeated then tucked her legs beneath her and snuggled close. "I haven't heard that phrase since I was a little girl."

Her foot struck her purse and it fell off the sofa, its contents scattering across the floor. When she attempted to sit up, Rory placed an arm across her chest, stopping her.

"I'll get it," he said, then bent and scooped the items back inside. "What's this?" he asked as he sat back, drawing her purse to his lap.

Macy glanced over and her smile faded when she

saw that he held the tin. "It's just something Sheila gave me," she said and reached to take it.

He turned a shoulder, blocking her and gave the tin a shake. "What's in it?"

"Just a bunch of old pictures of Sheila and my mother."

"Have you looked at them?"

"Briefly."

"Mind if I take a look?"

Before she could stop him, he'd lifted the lid. She slumped back against the sofa in a huff. "Like it would matter if I'd said no."

He picked up a picture and whistled through his teeth. "Wow. Is that your mother?"

She spared the photo a glance. "Yeah."

"Man, she was a looker."

"Her one positive attribute."

Rory heard the resentment in her voice and wondered what had happened between the two that had left her so bitter. "Tell me about her."

"Beautiful. Selfish. Demanding." She opened a hand and let it drop. "That pretty much sums her up."

He shook his head. "And they say opposites attract."

She looked at him askance.

"Change *beautiful* to *handsome*," he said, "and you could've been describing my father."

She eased around, her curiosity aroused. "Do you look like him?"

He smoothed a hand over his jaw and preened. "So you think I'm handsome, do you?"

"Only *you* would be able to pluck a compliment out of my question."

Chuckling, he rested the tin on his lap and draped an arm along the sofa behind her. "Yeah, I favor him. In fact all of my brothers do, though not as strongly as I do. But we all inherited his black hair and blue eyes."

"You and your brothers do resemble one another, yet you're all so different. In build *and* personality."

He snorted a laugh. "You can say that again. Woodrow's by far the biggest. Ry was always the smartest, made the best grades. And Ace…well, he's a saint as far as I'm concerned. Don't misunderstand," he was quick to tell her. "He can be as big a pain in the butt as the rest of 'em. But it was Ace who raised us. After our mother died, he stepped in and took charge. Made sure we ate our vegetables, washed behind our ears." He chuckled at a long-forgotten memory. "And gave us lickings when he thought we needed 'em."

"Why didn't your father do those things?"

"Buck?" He shook his head. "He was too busy carousing to spend any time at home."

Frowning thoughtfully, she took the tin from him and shuffled through the pictures. "I wonder if he's in any of these."

He shifted closer to peer over her shoulder. "If there was a party goin' on, you can bet Buck was there. That one," he said, and reached to pull a picture from the stack she held. He sank back, staring. "Yep. That's the old man, all right."

"Let me see." Drawing her legs beneath her, she took the picture from him. "They definitely look like they're having a good time,'' she said, then glanced over at him. ''Do you recognize any of the other people?''

He leaned close. ''Some.'' He pointed to one. ''That guy there is Bill Schueler. The one behind him is Tom Carey. And I believe that one,'' he said, pointing to a man holding a beer mug high, ''is J. W. Fielding.''

He didn't bother to mention that it was his father sitting center front, or that it was Darla Jean on his father's lap. He figured Macy would recognize her own mother, and the resemblance between him and his old man was strong enough for her to pick him out of the crowd.

He stole a glance her way and saw the wistful way in which she looked at the picture. What did she wish for? he wondered. That things had worked out differently? That her mother had married the man who had fathered her? That she had grown up knowing both her mother and her father? That her mother had been a loving and giving woman, rather than the selfish and demanding one Macy had described?

But there was no sense in wishing for things that couldn't be. You couldn't change the past. Rory had tried and failed enough times to know it couldn't be done.

He brushed a lock of her hair back from her cheek and tucked it behind her ear. ''What are you thinking?'' he asked quietly.

His voice seemed to draw her from a place far away. She heaved a sigh, then shook her head. ''Nothing really. Just…thinking.''

''You are who you are, Macy,'' he told her, sure

that he knew her thoughts. "It doesn't matter what your mother was like or who your father was. None of that changes who you are."

She angled her head to look at him. "And who is that?"

Though he might have expected it, he heard no sarcasm in her tone, saw no resentment in the eyes that searched his. Only a sincere desire to know. His smile tender, he curved his fingers around the back of her neck. "I'll tell you who you are. You're Macy Keller. A damn good landscape architect. An independent woman who can be stubborn to the point of downright mule-headedness at times. You're honest. Fair. Talented. Creative. Generous." He took a breath, then released it and slid farther down on the sofa, putting himself eye level with her. "And a wild-cat in bed."

She dropped her gaze to hide a smile. "That's a line of bull, if ever I heard one."

He crooked a knuckle beneath her chin and forced her face to his. "I've been known to blow a little smoke now and again," he admitted. "But what I said just now is the God's truth. You're all those things and more."

She narrowed an eye. "Even that part about being a wildcat in bed?"

Chuckling, he dragged her across his lap. "Especially that part."

Pressing a finger against the middle of his chest, she drew slow circles with her nail. "Are you planning on staying the night?"

"I could, or we can go to my place."

She snuggled close and tipped her face up to his. "I'd rather stay here, if that's okay."

He thought of the king-size bed and Jacuzzi tub at his apartment and compared it to the matchbox-size bed and telephone-booth-size shower her trailer offered.

Sliding an arm beneath her knees, he stood and lifted her high on his chest. "Fine by me."

She wrapped her arms around his neck. "Good, because I want you naked *now*."

Laughing, he strode the three steps it took to reach her bed. "Kinda bossy, aren't you?" he challenged as he opened his arms and let her fall.

She rolled to her knees and reached for his belt. "Is that a complaint?"

"Hell, no." He dragged his tie over his head and went to work on the buttons of his shirt. "I admire a woman who isn't afraid to speak her mind."

"Then I guess it wouldn't offend you if I were to tell you that you've got a really cute butt."

In the midst of shucking off his shirt, he stopped and looked at her closely. "Exactly how many glasses of champagne did you have?"

Her smile coy, she slipped her fingers into the waistband of his slacks and tugged him toward her. "I don't know. Every time I took a sip, your brothers were filling up my glass again."

He pushed her back to the bed and followed her down, burying his face in the valley between her breasts. "Remind me to thank them tomorrow."

Laughing, she dragged his face up to hers. "But then they'll want to know what you're thanking them for."

"They won't need to." He nipped at her lips. "One look at the smile on my face and they'll know."

The next morning, Rory sat opposite Macy at the narrow table in her trailer, sipping coffee, the pictures from the tin scattered on the tabletop between them.

"They sure seemed to party a lot," he commented as he laid aside one picture and picked up another.

"And pretty much with the same group of people," she added.

"I suppose it's possible that one of these men is your father."

"I suppose," she said, then dropped her chin onto her hand. "But how am I going to figure out which one? Nobody wants to talk to me about my mother, and the ones who are willing don't know anything."

Hearing the futility in her voice, Rory tried to think of a way to cheer her up. "You'll find him," he assured her. "It's just going to take time, is all."

She dropped her hand in frustration. "But I can't hang around here forever."

He stiffened at the thought of her leaving, something he hadn't given thought to in a while. "Why not?"

"I have to work. I've been living off the profit from the sale of my business, but I can't do that much longer. I'll need start-up money for a new business, once I've decided where I want to settle down."

He opened his hands. "Why not stay here? Tanner's Crossing could use a good landscape architect. The only one we've got spends more time in the Bahamas than he does working."

She huffed a breath. "That man would deserve to

lose his business to me, after leaving you with a parking lot of wilting plants.''

"Damned right he would," he said, anxious to persuade her to stay. "There's plenty of commercial property for sale around town. I'd imagine the Tanners own a piece or two of it and would be willing to cut you a fair price, considering you're a friend of the family.''

Her smile faded at the reminder of what had brought her to Tanner's Crossing. "I don't know," she said hesitantly. "I left Dallas, intending to start over somewhere new. Someplace where I wouldn't bump into memories of my mother at every turn. If I relocated here, it seems I would be defeating my purpose, as I'd be right in the middle of her old stomping grounds.''

"It's not like you have to decide right now," he said and started gathering up the pictures and dumping them back into the tin. "You'll have plenty of time to think it over while you're doing the work out at my place.''

With the grand opening of his store out of the way and a manager in place to run it, Rory could turn his full attention to the construction of his house. He was anxious for the house to be completed so that he could say farewell to apartment living.

At least he'd say farewell to the apartment he rented in Tanner's Crossing. He planned to hold on to the other five he kept in the cities where his stores were located, as they provided him a place to stay when he was making the circuit, checking on his businesses.

But for now, his focus was on his new home.

As he walked through the kitchen, he stopped to admire the new commercial range that had been installed. He wasn't much of a cook himself, but he figured when he entertained, whatever caterer he hired would make good use of the equipment. Giving the range a proud pat he moved on, passing through the open back door to check on Macy.

He stopped and grinned when he spotted her, stretched out on the hammock he'd hung between two trees. "Caught you sleepin' on the job," he said as he crossed to her.

She glanced up from the sketchbook she held propped up on her knees, then back down, hiding a smile. "Don't even think about docking my pay. I'm just taking advantage of the shade while I work on your design."

He gave her a nudge, indicating for her to scoot over, then stretched out on the hammock beside her. Folding an arm behind his head, he strained to look at the drawing, but she braced the side of her hand on the edge of the pad, blocking his view.

"Hey," he complained. "I can't see."

Ignoring him, she continued to sketch. "And you won't until I'm done. I don't like for my customers to see my designs before they're finished."

"But I'm not a regular customer."

"What are you, then?"

He nuzzled her neck. "Your lover?" he suggested hopefully. "Surely that should earn me a few perks."

She batted a hand at his head, then resumed her sketching. "Sorry, Romeo. Just because you're good in the sack doesn't mean you get special treatment."

"Then you can forget me spending the night at your place tonight."

She lifted an unconcerned shoulder. "Just means more room in the bed for me."

Since threats hadn't worked, he gave her his most pitiful puppy-dog look. "Come on, Macy," he wheedled. "Just one little peek. What would it hurt?"

She glanced his way, then huffed a breath. "Oh, for heaven's sake," she said, and handed over the pad. "You can be such a baby."

Smug, he took the pad from her and looked over the design. "What's this?" he asked, pointing to a series of circles that ended in a square near the patio that extended off the master bedroom.

"A waterfall and koi pond. You can nix it if you want. It's just an idea I had. I thought it would be cool if you could hear the sound of running water from your bedroom."

"It would," he agreed, liking the idea. "And this?" he asked, indicating a rougher drawing in the margin.

Macy glanced over, then quickly away, having forgotten about the fanciful sketch she'd made while daydreaming. "It's nothing. Just an idea I was playing around with."

He scooted closer and bumped her shoulder. "Tell me about it."

She kept her face turned away, embarrassed beyond belief. She rarely gave in to romantic daydreams and couldn't believe that he'd seen the product of this one, especially since she'd had the two of them in mind while weaving it.

"It's nothing. Really. You probably wouldn't like it, anyway."

"How will you know unless you tell me what it is?"

She grabbed the pad and furiously rubbed the eraser end of her pencil over the sketch. "It was a dumb idea, okay? While I was drawing in the koi pond, I came up with the crazy notion that you would get more use out of it if it was designed as an outdoor shower and hot tub." She swept away the rubbings, threw down the pencil, then folded her arms across her chest and turned her face away. "Like I said, it was a dumb idea."

"I don't think it's dumb at all," he said, studying the rough sketch. "In fact, I kinda like it. Reminds me of those old Tarzan movies Johnny Weissmuller starred in. I remember watching one where he and Jane were playing around underneath a waterfall. If I remember correctly, he and Jane ended up doing the tango for two in the pool. Of course, that was only the impression that was given. Back then sex scenes were a big no-no on the big screen."

He chuckled. "I kinda like the idea of me playing Tarzan under a waterfall with a naked Jane. Sliding down into the pool when things get all hot and heavy and making love in the water." He shivered. "Kind of turns me on just thinking about it."

She swung her legs over the side of the hammock and stalked away. "Yeah. I'm sure all your Janes will love it, too."

"Hey!" he called after her. "Where are you going?"

"To work," she called over her shoulder. She

snatched a tree pruner from the stack of tools she'd propped against the garage wall and ducked around the side of the house.

Stopping beneath a redbud tree, she whacked off a damaged limb and silently cursed herself for ever drawing the stupid waterfall in the first place, then lopped off another and cursed herself some more for placing herself in the scene with Rory.

Hearing him describe the fantasy she'd envisioned with a generic ''Jane'' had served as a brutal reminder that he might be her Tarzan, but she wasn't the only ''Jane'' in his life.

Rory was a womanizer. A flirt. She'd tagged him as one the first time they'd met. And she had his sister-in-law to thank for confirming her suspicions for her. But she'd never thought that it would hurt so much to think about him being with another woman.

''Get over it,'' she told herself, and stooped to gather up the limbs she'd pruned. She was a big girl. She knew the rules of survival in the dating game. You took what you could get, enjoyed it while you had it, then moved on and never looked back when it was over.

But this time, when it was over, she had a feeling she was going to find it a lot harder not to look back.

Her arms full, she turned to carry the limbs to the brush pile she'd started earlier and bumped into something hard. She backed up a step and lowered the limbs to find Rory standing in front of her.

''Was it something I said?'' he asked.

She gulped, swallowed, then shook her head and darted around him. ''It was time for me to get back to work. I don't have time to loll around, chewing the fat with you.'' She dumped the limbs onto the pile, then headed for her Jeep. ''I'm going to town and grab a bite to eat. Do you want me to bring you something back?''

He reached around her and opened her door. ''I've got a better idea.''

Unaware that he'd followed her, she stepped back, wiping her hands down the sides of her overalls. ''What?''

''Let's go over to Ry's and raid his refrigerator, then come back here and have a picnic.''

''You can't just go barging into someone's house and steal their food!''

''Why not? He's my brother. He won't care.''

Before she could think of another excuse to avoid sharing a picnic with him, she found herself behind the wheel of her Jeep and Rory climbing into the passenger seat beside her.

Seven

Macy tramped along behind Rory, still sulking over the fact that he'd outmaneuvered her.

"If you'd told me you were planning on having this picnic in the Big Thicket," she grumbled, "I'd never have agreed to come along."

"You didn't agree," he reminded her. "But don't worry. We're almost there."

"And exactly where is *there?* We've been walking for hours."

He stopped and waited for her to catch up. "It hasn't been hours. Fifteen minutes, tops."

She braced a hand on his shoulder and lifted a foot. "Feels like hours," she muttered as she ripped off a prickly vine that had attached itself to her sock.

Chuckling, he strode on, swinging the picnic basket in his right hand while balancing a rolled-up blanket on his shoulder with his left.

Curling her lip in a snarl, Macy stalked after him. But it wasn't long before she was lagging behind again. She lost sight of him when he stepped into a thick grouping of trees. She quickened her step, not at all sure she could find her way back to his house without him. Weaving her way through the trees, she stepped out into a small clearing, where she found Rory spreading the blanket beneath the shade of a mammoth live oak.

Frowning, she looked around. "Are we still on your land?"

"Not mine, specifically, but it's Tanner land."

Though she'd never admit it, the spot he'd chosen for their picnic was idyllic, a picturesque setting straight from the pages of a magical fairy tale. Trees a hundred or more years old towered overhead, their lattice of limbs creating a cool oasis of shade. Wildflowers peeked from beneath the drooping blades of the native grasses that carpeted the area, their colorful blooms looking like confetti sprinkled across the ground.

Her curiosity peaked by the sound of running water, Macy went in search of it. She didn't have to look far. A creek ran through the grove of trees not far beyond, its water crystal clear. Rocks chipped from the walls of the creek's banks by time and weather formed crude dams, which in turn formed deep pools. Water churned and gurgled in the recesses between the rocks before tumbling over them, creating a symphony of sound that filled the woods.

"Pretty neat, huh?"

She jumped, startled, then frowned, unaware that Rory had followed her. "Yeah. I suppose."

"Want to go for a swim?"

She glanced back at him in alarm. "Here?"

Grinning, he tugged his T-shirt from the waist of his jeans and dragged it over his head. "Why not?"

She wiped her hands across the seat of her overalls, while trying her darnedest not to look at his chest. "Sorry, but I don't have a suit."

He unfastened his belt buckle while toeing off his boots. "You don't need one. It's just you and me here."

She gulped, watching as he pushed his jeans down his legs, then turned away, squeezing her eyes shut against the tempting sight of his nude body. "I'm really not much of a swimmer."

She felt his hands light on her shoulders, then the warmth of his breath against her neck. A split second later his lips touched her there.

"Who said anything about swimming?"

The huskiness in his voice, the suggestion in it, turned her knees to jelly. "Rory," she began.

He eased the straps of her overalls over her shoulders, then pressed his lips to the skin he'd exposed and dragged the straps down her arms. "Yeah?"

"I—" She gulped as he slid his arms around her waist and drew her back against him.

"This is what you were thinking about, wasn't it?" he murmured against her ear. "When you were drawing that sketch, you were thinking about you and me standing beneath the waterfall and making love in the pool."

Stunned, she turned slowly in his arms. "You knew?"

Smiling softly, he swept a lock of hair from her

cheek and tucked it behind her ear. "I may be slow, but I'm not completely dense." He dropped his hands to her waist and gave her overalls the encouragement they needed to clear her hips. Teasing her lips with his, he slipped his hands beneath her tank top and stroked his palms up, flicking his thumbs over her nipples before pulling the top up and over her head.

He stooped, catching her beneath her knees and hefting her up into his arms. "Better lose those shoes if you don't want them to get wet," he warned as he started down the bank.

Clinging to his neck with one arm, Macy quickly yanked off her shoes and socks, then locked her hands around his neck as he made his way across the moss-covered rocks to a boulder lodged midstream.

"Ready?" he asked.

She drew in a breath, held it, gave a quick nod. He stepped off the rock and plunged them into the water. The shock of the cold water had her clinging tighter to his neck as they drifted to the bottom. He held her against him and kicked, forcing them back up.

As they broke through the surface, Macy slicked her hair back from her face, laughing. "This is insane," she cried, then squealed as he lifted her high in the air and planted a kiss on her belly button, before plunking her down on the boulder.

Laughing, she shook out her hair, watching as he heaved himself from the water. Her laughter faded as he swung himself around to sit beside her, the muscles on his arms and chest cording at the effort. Droplets of water dripped from his chin and hair and ran in glistening rivulets down his chest. Her heart pounding, she lifted her gaze to his and found him watching her. Eyes as blue as the sky overhead and fathomless as the sea seemed to draw her in, hold her.

I'm falling in love with this man.

The realization sucked the breath from her lungs, twisted her gut with panic, yet she couldn't deny the emotions that swelled inside her as he lifted a hand to cup her cheek. His lips, as they touched hers, were cold from the water, yet warmed quickly, as did her body, at the gentle stroking of his hands.

She wanted to freeze this moment, keep it with her always so that she could remember this feeling, the pure unadulterated joy of experiencing love for the first time. But her need for him, the desperate yearning to have him inside her, to be physically joined with him, superceded all else, and she sank back with him to lie on the boulder, twining her legs with his, seeking and exploring his body with her hands while he did the same to hers. His touch was that of a master, each stroke of his fingers over her flesh filling her with color and light and a heat that licked higher and higher. It burned behind her eyes, seared her throat, churned in her belly, until she was desperate to have him inside her, feel the stretch of her flesh, the exquisite pressure as he filled her.

But first she wanted to touch him, taste him.

Curling her hand around his erection, she stroked her fingers slowly down to the nest of dark hair at its base, up to swirl the tip of one finger in the pearl of moisture that formed at its head, then down again, smearing the moisture along his shaft. She kept her touch light, her strokes slow and even, though there was a need in her for speed, for greed.

When she was unable to resist any longer, she

pulled her mouth from his and slid down his body, raining kisses over his chest and abdomen in her journey down. He jerked reflexively as she closed her lips around him, then fisted his hands in her hair and groaned as she took him deep. She felt the power in him, the heat and a need that equaled her own.

She lifted her gaze to his and he reached for her, pulling her over him and fitting her knees against his hips. Holding her in place by the strength of his gaze alone, he slipped his fingers between her legs, spread her feminine lips and guided his sex to her opening. Her breath caught in her lungs at the heat, the pressure. Before she could draw another, he linked his hands with hers and drew her down, bringing her mouth to his as he stretched his arms above his head, pinning her hands against the stone.

"Ride me," he whispered against her lips. "Ride me as fast and as hard as you want."

Heat shot through her body at the invitation, and she pushed her hips into the curve of his groin, taking him in. With an abandon that she'd never experienced with any other man, she rode him, taking him deeper and deeper and faster and faster with each rise and fall of her hips, racing frantically toward a satisfaction that danced maddeningly just out of her reach. Frustrated, she tore her hands from his and used them to brace herself against his chest as she ground her hips against his.

A tremble started at her toes and climbed upward, increasing in power and intensity until it shattered in her womb and exploded in a kaleidoscope of color behind her eyes. Her muscles burning, her lungs screaming for air, she held herself rigid against him, wanting to draw every ounce of pleasure that she could from him, give him all the pleasure he deserved in return.

As if knowing her thoughts, her needs, he sat up and wrapped his arms around her like a vise, holding her to him. She felt the shudder that ripped through him, the spasm of his sex inside her, and she buried her face in the curve of his neck and shattered a second time.

He continued to hold her against him, his hands stroking over her back while their bodies cooled, then pressed his lips in the curve of her neck. "You okay?"

Weak, sated, deliriously happy, she couldn't find the words to tell him that she was more than okay. Instead, she drew back and framed his face with her hands.

"If this is what water does to you, you can forget the koi pond. I'm building you a creek right through the middle of your house."

Chuckling, he pushed off the boulder and slid down into the water, holding her close. "I figured I could make you see things my way."

"This is a family dinner," Macy continued to argue stubbornly as Rory drove to the ranch for Sunday dinner at Ry's. "You told me so yourself. I'm not family, so I shouldn't have to go."

"Don't you like my family?"

Folding her arms across her chest, she turned her face to the passenger window. "They're all right, I guess."

"Then what's the problem? It's not like you're

crashing. I was given strict instructions to bring you with me.''

"But it's a family dinner!" she cried. "Why would they want me there, when I'm not family?''

"So they'll have someone to chuck food at?'' He tossed up a hand. "Hell, I don't know. I guess it's because they like you.''

Moaning pitifully, she slumped farther down in her seat. "I'll probably make a fool of myself,'' she said miserably.

"It's not like you're having dinner with the royal family,'' he told her. "We're just normal folks getting together for Sunday dinner. Didn't you and your family ever do that?''

She spared him a look. "You're kidding, right? My family consisted of a stepfather who barely tolerated me, a mother who wished I'd never been born and me.'' Frowning, she turned to face the windshield again. "We barely spoke, much less shared a meal.''

Finally understanding why she'd kicked up such a fuss about having dinner with his family, Rory reached across the console and squeezed her hand. "You'll do all right,'' he assured her. "My family likes you.'' Biting back a smile, he returned his hand to the wheel and added, "Though I can't understand why.''

"Hey!'' she cried defensively. "There's nothing wrong with me.''

"Did I say there was?''

"You said you didn't know why your family liked me, which is the same darn thing.''

Chuckling, he pulled his truck in behind Woodrow's and shut off the engine. "I was just trying to get a rise out of you."

She shoved open the door. "Congratulations," she grumbled, then slammed it. "You did an excellent job."

Trying to hide his amusement, Rory trailed her up the walkway. When she hesitated at the door, he reached around her to push it open. "No need to knock," he said, and gave her a nudge. "They're expecting us."

"Seems as if we've done this before," she muttered, then stepped inside.

"Is that a roast I smell?" Rory called as he urged her down the long hall and into the kitchen.

"I swear that boy's got a nose like a bloodhound," Woodrow groused.

"Boy!" Rory repeated, then put up his fists and danced around his brother, punching at air. "Better watch who you call 'boy,'" he warned. "You're liable to get the tar beat out of you."

In a surprisingly smooth move for a man of his size, Woodrow caught Rory in a headlock and bent him double, scrubbing his knuckles over his hair. "I'd like to see you try."

"Cut it out, you two," Maggie scolded. "You know the rules. No fighting in the house."

Woodrow released Rory, mumbling, "Sorry."

Grinning, Rory shot Maggie a wink. "I'm sure Woodrow will thank you later for saving him from a whipping." He held out his hands to the baby Maggie held on her hip. "Come here, sweet cheeks, and give your uncle Rory a big kiss."

Macy hung back, watching in amazement at the ease with which Rory handled the baby.

He glanced her way. "You remember Laura, don't you?" he asked, then blew a raspberry kiss on the infant's cheek, making her laugh, before thrusting her at Macy. "Hold her a minute, would you? I need to kiss the cook."

Stunned to find herself with a baby in her arms, Macy stared at the infant, then shifted her gaze, watching as Rory scooped Ry's wife off her feet to plant a loud, smacking kiss full on her mouth.

"I swear, Kayla, you get prettier every day," he said, as he set her on her feet again. He slung an arm around her shoulders and leaned to sniff the air above the skillet she'd been stirring. "Mmm-mmm," he hummed lustily. "Red-eye gravy. If Ry hadn't already staked his claim on you, I'd drop down on a knee and propose."

"Hey," Ry cried indignantly. "That's my wife you're groping."

His hands in the air, Rory backed away. "Just giving the cook the appreciation she deserves," he said, then looked around expectantly. "So, when do we eat? I'm starving."

The baby chose that moment to grab Macy's necklace. Instinctively, she closed her hand over the baby's, keeping her from breaking the chain.

Chuckling, Maggie reached for her daughter. "Here. I'll take her." She shifted the baby to a hip, then looped an arm around Macy's waist and gave her a squeeze. "I know they can seem a bit overwhelming at first, but you'll get used to it."

*   *   *

Dazed, Macy sat at the table between Rory and Woodrow, having given up any hope of eating. With six different conversations going on at the same time, her head spun dizzily at the effort of trying to follow them all. The Tanners, from what she'd been able to determine, were loud, opinionated and openly affectionate.

She couldn't decide whether she wanted to run screaming from the room or beg them to let her move in.

She felt Rory's hand on her knee and glanced his way.

Hiding a smile, he leaned close. "Still wish I'd let you stay at the trailer?"

She let out a nervous breath. "Ask me that again later. The jury's still out."

Chuckling, he draped an arm along her chair's back and gave her neck a squeeze then he turned his attention to Ace, who was in a heated debate with Ry over whether or not children should be allowed to legally divorce themselves from their parents. Though Rory seemed totally absorbed in the conversation he gently massaged the taut muscles in her neck. The gesture seemed so unconscious, so natural, Macy doubted he was even aware of his hand's movement. But she was. So much so, it took her a moment to realize that the conversation at the table had stopped and everyone was looking at her expectantly.

She darted a panicked glance at Rory.

"Ace asked if you'd had any luck finding your father," he said.

Her face heating in embarrassment, she offered Ace

a weak smile. "Sorry. My mind must've wandered for a minute. And, no, I haven't found him yet."

"Any leads?" he asked.

"Nothing that's paid off. Dixie gave me the name of a woman my mother ran around with. Sheila Tompkins. I met with her, but she had nothing to offer other than a tin of old photos. It seems that no one was aware that my mother was pregnant when she left Tanner's Crossing."

Frowning, Ace glanced at Ry. "What about medical records? If Macy's mother's pregnancy was confirmed by a local doctor, wouldn't there be some kind of record of that?"

"I'd imagine so," Ry replied.

"But even if the medical records exist," Elizabeth interjected, "their contents are confidential and can't be shared without the written consent of the patient."

"And since Macy's mother is deceased," Ry surmised, "finding out what is inside those records would be impossible."

Ace lifted a brow and looked down his nose at Elizabeth and Ry. "It wouldn't be if we could find us a doctor who was willing to bend a few rules."

When Elizabeth and Ry remained stoically silent, Ace huffed a breath. "You two are disgustingly honest. What we need in this family is a crooked lawyer."

Woodrow lifted a brow. "Is there any other kind?"

Macy sat at the narrow kitchen table, the photos spread before her. The discussion with Rory's family about her family had prompted her to draw the photos out again. She held a pencil poised over a legal pad, having divided the page into two columns. Names filled half of the left column. The right was reserved for an *X,* once Macy eliminated the man as a possibility.

"Do you have any idea how long it's going to take to find all these men?" Rory asked in frustration. "There must be fifty names on the list already and we haven't even gone through half the pictures."

"Do you have a better idea?"

Exhausted, he dropped his forehead to rest on the arms he'd folded on the table. "No," he mumbled. "But there's got to be a better way."

"When you come up with one, let me know. Until you do, I'm working on this list."

Moaning pitifully, he lifted his head. "Please," he begged. "No more tonight. I've looked at these pictures so long, all the faces are beginning to look the same."

Though she hated to quit, when there were more pictures to examine and men to identify, Macy heard the exhaustion in Rory's voice and laid down her pencil. Rising, she offered him her hand. "Come on, Romeo. Let's go to bed."

He dropped his hand into hers and let her tug him to his feet.

Chuckling, she steered him toward the bunk. "Why are you more tired than I am? You're working on the same amount of sleep that I got last night."

He lolled his head and gave her a pained look. "Obviously you've forgotten the game of touch football I played with my brothers after dinner and the hours I spent crawling around on the floor like a horse, with my niece perched on my back."

"Poor baby," she murmured sympathetically as she unfastened his jeans. "And to think your team lost, too."

"We wouldn't have if Woodrow had any kind of arm. The passes he threw to me were a good ten feet over my head."

Trying not to laugh, she dragged his jeans down his legs, then held them open while he stepped out of them. "Maybe you should've played quarterback and let Woodrow be the receiver."

"It wouldn't have done any good. He's got hands like hams. Couldn't hold on to a ball if it was super-glued to his palms."

Rising, she caught the hem of his T-shirt and peeled it up and over his head. "He can't help it that he's big. Inside or out?" she asked as she draped his clothes over a hook on the wall.

"Inside," he said, and crawled onto the narrow bunk, claiming the space closest to the wall. Collapsing onto his back, he dropped an arm over his eyes with a sigh.

Smiling, Macy slid beneath the sheet and snuggled up against him. "'Night, Rory."

He rolled to his side and hooked an arm over her waist, tugged her up close. "'Night," he murmured sleepily as he wove his legs through hers.

His next breath was a soft snore.

Macy stared at his face in the darkness and slowly reached to comb a tendril of hair from his forehead, emotion filling her throat. How had this happened? she wondered. She'd known him only a few short weeks, yet there was a casualness between them, an ease, that took most couples months to develop, if not years. The way he sought her feet with his beneath the covers…the way he held her hugged up against his chest, as if they'd been sleeping together for years, instead of mere days.

She smiled and smoothed a finger across his brow, knowing it was Rory who made things so easy. She'd never experienced this kind of naturalness with a man before. Had never known to even expect it. Her past relationships with men had been anything but memorable. Bumped noses during a kiss. Not knowing where to put your hands or whether you really wanted to put them anywhere at all. Faking an orgasm just to put an end to the misery. Suffering through the dreaded morning-after awkwardness and wondering why you'd ever agreed to stay the night in the first place.

With Rory, it was different. Everything with him was easy. Natural. Enjoyable. Breathtaking. They just seemed to fit. Which in itself was a concern.

She was already aware that she was falling in love with him, which she knew was a mistake but seemed to have no control over. He'd never voiced his feelings for her, never mentioned anything about the future. He seemed perfectly content to continue as they were, seeped in an affair that they both obviously enjoyed. Not so long ago, Macy wouldn't have had a problem with that. Her mother and stepfather's marriage hadn't exactly been an advertisement for wedded bliss. They had fought and quarreled, seeming to find their only pleasure in making the other unhappy. As a result, she had never sought marriage and was content to live her life alone.

But that was before she'd met Rory, before she'd

experienced the warmth of his comfort, the security she'd found in having him there when she needed him most, the joy she'd discovered in exploring his body and having him explore hers. And that was before she'd met his family. Experienced the warmth and fun that came with being a part of such a large, extended group. Before she'd known what it was like to hold a child in her arms, feel a baby's tiny fingers wrapped around hers, seen the innocence, the trust in an infant's eyes, as they looked into hers.

Before, her yearnings had been nothing but fantasies, dreams she'd created in her mind, not a reality she ever saw for herself. But now she knew that it was possible to love and feel love in return. That squabbling and fussing weren't part of a family's normal routine, a way of life that constantly threatened the foundation of the home and the lives of those who lived within it.

And now she wanted a husband and family.

Pensive, she drew a finger along Rory's cheek, wondering if he wanted those things, too, and if he did, would he want them with her. He'd once suggested that she stay in Tanner's Crossing, set up her business here. But that wasn't a proposal. Maybe he'd only suggested it as a convenient way to have her close by.

But what would happen if he should grow tired of her? How would she ever be able to live in the same town and see him with other women when she loved him so much?

Groaning, she turned her face into her pillow. You're being ridiculous, she told herself. You're worrying about things that you have no business even thinking about. Her relationship with Rory was new. They were only just beginning to get to know each other. Only time would tell whether or not his feelings for her were the same as hers for him.

A phone rang, its shrill sound piercing the quiet. Already awake, the sound merely startled Macy. But Rory sat bolt upright, bumping his head on the low ceiling over the bunk.

"Damn," he swore, rubbing his head, then crawling over her to search for his cell phone in the tangle of clothes on the floor. Finding it, he sank back on the edge of the bed and drew the phone to his ear. "Tanner," he said wearily.

Scooting back to give him room, Macy curled herself around him, resting her head on his back.

"What!" he cried.

Startled by the alarm she heard in his voice, Macy reached to turn on the wall lamp at the head of the bed.

Rory listened a moment, frowning. "No, no," he said. "You were right to call me." He stood and dragged a hand over his hair. "Call a roofing contractor and get him over there, as quick as you can. Offer to pay him double if you have to. Then get a salvage crew in and have them start pumping out the water." He turned his wrist and checked the time. "I should be able to make it there by daylight, if not before. I'll take care of the rest when I do."

He disconnected the call and started gathering his clothes.

"What happened?" Macy asked.

"Roof collapsed on my store in Houston. Rained six inches or more within the space of a couple of hours. Roof couldn't take the weight and broke through. Water's standing knee-deep in the store.''

She swung her legs over the side of the bed as he started down the short hall, tugging on his jeans. ''Is there anything I can do?''

He stopped and whipped on his shirt, then turned and dropped a kiss on her mouth. ''No, but thanks for offering.''

He stooped to tug on his boots, then grabbed his hat and reached for the door. ''I'll give you a call. Let you know what's happenin'.'' He opened the door, then glanced back. ''I don't want you out at the house while I'm gone.''

''Rory—''

He pressed a finger against her lips. ''Don't argue,'' he ordered. ''Once I get back and make sure the men understand that you're the boss, then you can get back to work. Until then, I want you stayin' clear of the place. Understand?''

Though it galled her to be told what to do, Macy held her tongue, figuring he had enough to worry about without having to worry about her, too. ''I understand,'' she assured him, then added, ''Be careful.''

He dropped another kiss on her mouth. ''I will.''

And then he was gone.

Eight

Since she wasn't allowed to do any work out at Rory's house, Macy had way too much time on her hands. Cleaning up the trailer took a nanosecond and without a TV to watch she quickly grew bored. Thinking she could pass some time by checking on the plants at Rory's store, she climbed into her Jeep and headed for town.

The parking lot was crowded—a good sign that his grand opening was a success—so she pulled her vehicle into a space near the back. Unwrapping a hose from the holder at the side of the building, she turned on the water and began her circuit, checking the plants for signs of disease and distress as she watered.

She'd just stepped around to the front when she noticed a man standing beneath one of the mountain laurels she'd planted between Rory's store and the one next door. He was tall, standing at least six feet or more and wore faded jeans and a long-sleeved work shirt. He wore a cap on his head that shadowed his face, and he appeared to have what looked like a knife in his hand.

Fearing he intended to carve his initials in the tree, without a thought for her own safety, Macy dropped the hose and ran. "Hey! What do you think you're doing?"

He whipped his head around, then quickly closed the blade and slipped the knife into his pocket.

He gestured to the tree's narrow trunk. "Bores," he said. "Noticed 'em when I drove up."

Sure that the man was lying, Macy squatted down to examine the trunk herself. It took her only a moment to find the tiny tunnels that indicated infestation. "I'll be darned," she murmured, then stood wiping her hands across the seat of her overalls. "I didn't notice anything wrong with the tree when I planted it."

"Doubt you would, seeing as the infestation just started."

"Yeah, but I pride myself on planting only healthy plants and my ability to detect one that isn't." She angled her head around to peer at him. "You've got a good eye. Better than mine, and that's saying something."

He ducked his head and looked away. "I've had more years."

She bit back a smile. The man talked in spurts, rather than sentences, but she found his manner of speech charming.

"Bet you bought them trees at the Plant Store," he said.

She looked at him in surprise. "How did you know that I did?"

"'Cause Arnold don't care about the reputation of his suppliers. Cheap is all that concerns him."

"Arnold," she repeated, frowning as she recognized the name of Rory's absentee landscaper. "If I'd known he was the one who owned the nursery, you can bet I'd never have darkened the door of his business."

"Hard not to, if you're wantin' to buy plants around here. His is the only place in town."

Intrigued by the odd man, she moved closer. "You seem to know an awful lot about plants."

Scraping the toe of his boot across the grass, he shrugged. "I've been known to dabble a bit. Got me a couple of greenhouses."

Greenhouses, Macy thought. Oh, how she missed hers. She stooped to pull a weed that had pushed up from between two squares of the freshly laid grass. "I had a nursery business in Dallas, but I sold it several months back. I've been giving some thought to opening one here."

"There's a need for a good one."

She glanced up to say something, but the words died in her throat when she found him staring at her chest. Pursing her lips, she clapped a hand over the exposed skin above her tank top.

His gaze shot to hers, then he looked away, his face turning a bright red. "Didn't mean no impropriety. Was admirin' your necklace, was all."

She eyed him a moment, trying to decide if he was

lying or not, then decided his embarrassment was real. Catching the locket between her fingers, she rose. "It was my mother's."

He nodded, but kept his gaze averted. "Looked to be an old one." He gestured toward the diseased tree. "You'll want to tend to that soon, 'fore it spreads."

She turned her gaze to the tree and frowned. "I hate to use chemicals, but then I'd hate to lose more of the trees."

"I've had some success with an organic mixture I concocted. I could bring you some, if you like."

She cocked her head curiously, thinking she may have just found a way to while away some of her time. "Do you live around here?"

"Not far."

"Why don't I follow you home and pick it up myself? It would give me an opportunity to see your greenhouses. If it wouldn't be an imposition," she added quickly.

His Adam's apple bobbed once, then he nodded and turned away. He lifted a hand, indicating a truck parked along the curb of the street. "Just keep your eye on Old Blue there."

Her request to see the man's greenhouses was impulsive, but not one Macy regretted making as she followed "Old Blue," as the man had referred to his truck, down a deeply rutted road. She supposed some would think her crazy to be following a complete stranger out into the boondocks, without knowing so much as his name. But Macy wasn't afraid. If anything, she was relieved to have something to do with her time. And spending time in a greenhouse was a much-missed pleasure.

She slowed when the truck ahead of her did, then turned onto the narrow lane behind it. Ahead she saw a small white-framed house. Surrounded by flowers and climbing vines of every description, it gleamed in the sunshine like the centerpiece of a colorful bouquet.

Charmed by the cottage-style garden, Macy parked her Jeep behind Old Blue and climbed down. "What a wonderful garden," she said as she crossed to peer over the low fence. "Yarrow, columbine, lavender, plumbago," she said, naming a few of the plants, then glanced back over her shoulder. "You've got quite a green thumb."

He gave his head a jerk. "Greenhouses are back here."

Macy hurried after him. After seeing the garden surrounding his house, she was anxious to see what kind of wonders his greenhouses held.

Two long buildings stood a hundred feet or more behind the house, their hinged windows open to the afternoon breeze. She followed the man through the doorway of the first greenhouse and stopped, her eyes rounding, as she looked around. Hanging baskets filled with every variety of blooming plant and fern imaginable hung from long iron pipes attached to the high ceiling. Beneath them, long wooden tables stretched along each side of the building and through its middle, leaving narrow walkways between. Macy walked down the nearest aisle, amazed by the number of plants crowded onto each. Vegetables. Herbs. Ferns. Vines. Each at different stages of development, they grew from a wide assortment of containers. Egg cartons. Sawed-off milk jugs. The standard plastic tray.

She turned. "This is amazing," she said, then laughed and clapped her hands to her cheeks. "No, it's mind-boggling. How do you manage to take care of all of these plants by yourself?"

He lifted a shoulder. "Just do." He pointed at a line of tubing that ran from one end of the building to the other with branches off to the sides. "Worked up a watering system. Makes tending 'em easy."

Fascinated, Macy followed the line of tubing, noting that each branch had smaller shoots of tubing feeding off it, whose ends were sunk into the dirt of each container. She had seen more elaborate systems, but it was obvious that this one was well designed. "You made this yourself?" she asked.

He nodded.

She pressed a finger into the soil of a container, testing its moisture. Nodding her approval, she dusted off her hands. "What about fertilization? How do you handle that?"

He motioned for her to follow him to a space near the door they'd entered where his watering system seemed to originate. Five-gallon jugs were upended on a long wooden shelf, their necks sunk into holes drilled into the wooden planks. Tubes ran from the mouth of each jug and were connected to the watering system by joints that looked like tiny spigots.

"Make my own fertilizer," he said, tapping a finger against the side of a jug filled with an amber liquid. "Call it Liquid Gold. Drain it off my compost piles. Provides all the nutrition my plants need."

Amazed by his creativity, as well as impressed with his obvious success, she turned to tell him so, but sputtered a laugh. "I don't even know your name." She offered him her hand. "I'm Macy Keller."

She watched the slow, hesitant drag of his hand up the side of his jeans before he took her hand in his.

"John. John Sullivan."

Later that evening, Macy lay stretched out on the lounge chair in the strip of grass in front of her trailer, her eyes closed, as she listened to the birds singing in the treetop overhead.

She was lonely, but it was a good kind of lonely, because she knew that it would end the second Rory returned from Houston. He had called earlier that afternoon to give her an update on the water damage at his Houston store and promised to call again later, to let her know when to expect him home. Not wanting to miss his call, she had her cell phone on her lap and close at hand.

She could barely wait to talk to him so that she could tell him about meeting John Sullivan and how seeing his greenhouses had made her start thinking that opening a nursery in Tanner's Crossing wasn't such a bad idea. She was even thinking of asking John to work for her. He obviously knew a lot about plants and could probably even teach her a few things. His shyness might be a problem, though, as he might not like working retail, since it would require him to deal with people on a daily basis.

But she was sure they could find a way to work around that, depending on how flexible John was. She could always put him in charge of the care of the plants and hire a manager to handle the retail end. He might even be willing to work with her on designs and installations. Judging by the appearance of his own gardens, he obviously had a knack for both.

Her phone rang and she snatched it up. "Hello?"

"Hey, Macy. It's Rory."

Warmed by the sound of his voice, she snuggled into the lounge chair. "You sound tired."

"I am. This place is a zoo. The whole town seems to be under water. I even saw some people rowing a boat down the street."

"Heavens!" she exclaimed, then laughed. "I hope you remembered to pack your rubber boots."

"I didn't pack anything. Drove straight here."

"Rory," she said, unable to contain her excitement any longer. "I met the most unusual man today. John Sullivan. He—"

"I hate to interrupt. But can this wait? I'm swamped here."

Her excitement melting, she said, "Well, yeah. Sure. When are you coming home?"

"That's just it. I'm not. At least not tonight. We're still pumping water out of the building and we're having trouble lining up a roofer. I'll call you tomorrow and let you know how things are going. Maybe I'll have a better idea then."

Though disappointed, she tried her best to hide it. "Try to stay dry."

"I will."

"Rory?" she said before he could hang up.

"Yeah?"

"I—" She caught her lip between her teeth, catching herself before the words "love you" slipped out.

"Be careful," she said instead.

"You do the same," he said, then broke the connection.

A knock on her trailer door had Macy lifting her head from the list of names she was working on. She never had visitors…other than the nosy lady across the street. Praying it wasn't her, she laid aside the legal pad and telephone book and rose to cross to the door.

Her eyes rounded when she found Elizabeth Tanner standing on the stoop. "Well, hi," she said in surprise.

Elizabeth winced. "Is this a bad time? I could come back later if it is."

Macy pushed the door wide. "Heavens, no," she said and laughed as she tugged Elizabeth inside. "In fact, once I get you in here, I might not let you leave. I've been bored out of my mind since Rory left."

"Rory's gone?"

"He's in Houston. There was a flood and the roof on his store collapsed. He says things are really a mess."

"Oh, dear. Does he need help? I'm sure Woodrow would be happy to drive down if Rory needs him."

"I honestly don't know whether he needs help or not. But I'll mention it to him when I talk to him. He's supposed to call sometime today and let me know when he's planning to come home." She glanced at her wristwatch and frowned. "Although I would've thought he'd call by now."

Realizing that they were both still standing, Macy

darted to shove the photos and phone book to the side of the sofa. "I'm sorry. Sit. Please. I apologize for the mess, but I'm living in pretty tight quarters at the moment."

Elizabeth glanced around as she sat down. "I think it's rather cozy. Woodrow's and my home is small. He built it himself."

"Really?" Macy said in surprise. "I didn't know Woodrow was a builder."

"He's not. And least not professionally. He simply likes to work with his hands. Do things himself. He's really quite talented."

"I guess it's convenient having a handyman around."

"Even more so when you consider the remoteness of our location."

Macy looked at her curiously. "You and Woodrow don't live on the ranch?"

"The home place?" At Macy's nod, Elizabeth shook her head. "No. We have our own ranch about twenty miles farther out."

"Since Ry lives there and Rory will be living nearby soon, I assumed that all the brothers lived on the ranch."

Chuckling, Elizabeth shook her head. "I don't think Tanner's Crossing would survive having all the brothers living here again. From what I've heard, they were fairly rowdy when they were growing up.

"Ace and Maggie live in Kerrville," she went on to explain, "although we're trying to persuade them to move closer. And Whit has his own place not too far away."

Smiling, Elizabeth reached over and gave Macy's knee a pat. "But I didn't come over here to gossip about the family. I came to tell you that I did a little detective work while I was at the clinic today. And please don't get your hopes up," she added quickly. "Because I'm not here to tell you that I've discovered who your father is. But I noticed Sunday that you seemed disappointed that your mother's medical records were confidential and I thought I'd take a peek at them, just on the off chance that they might offer information that you might find useful."

"And?" Macy prodded.

"The only thing I can tell you is that your mother was definitely pregnant when she left Tanner's Crossing. There was a notation of a positive test in her file. Unfortunately the father's name wasn't listed."

Macy dropped her gaze to hide her disappointment. "I appreciate you looking. I know that you stretched the rules to do that."

Elizabeth draped an arm around her and hugged her to her side. "I wanted to help. I know it must be frustrating for you to keep constantly hitting dead ends."

Macy glanced at the pile of photos and the list of names she was working on. "That would be putting it mildly."

Elizabeth glanced at the pile of pictures Macy had shoved aside. "Are those the photos your mother's friend gave to you?"

"Yeah. I've made a list of all the men Rory recognized in the pictures and now I'm looking up their names in the telephone directory."

Elizabeth looked at her in surprise. "You plan to call them on the phone?"

Macy shook her head. "No. Although that was my intention when I began the list," she admitted. "But then I started thinking about the men's wives, their families, and realized how embarrassing, how potentially disastrous it would be, if I were to call and start asking a lot of questions about the past."

Elizabeth blew out a breath. "I see what you mean." She picked up a photo from the pile, then glanced at Macy. "Do you mind?" she asked.

Macy opened a hand. "Help yourself."

Elizabeth studied the photo and smothered a laugh. "Oh, my. Would you look at the style of their clothing?"

Macy scooted over so that she could see, too. "Yeah. They're pretty funny-looking. The amazing thing is those styles are coming back."

Elizabeth shuddered. "Maybe for some. Personally I wouldn't be caught dead wearing a skirt that short." She replaced the photo and picked up another. Her smile turned wistful. "Look," she said and pointed to a man who stood off a ways from the group. "He reminds me of Whit."

Frowning, Macy looked more closely at the photo, then shook her head. "I don't really remember what Whit looks like. I only saw him that one time."

"I didn't mean in looks," Elizabeth said. "It's as if he's standing on the outside, looking in. Obviously with the group, but not a part. Whit's like that."

"Rory said nearly the same thing."

"Rory said what same thing?"

Macy snapped up her head, then shot off the sofa when she saw Rory standing in the doorway. Laughing, he scooped her up in his arms and kissed her hard.

Elizabeth set the photo aside and stood, delicately clearing her throat.

Rory tore his mouth from Macy's long enough to shoot Elizabeth a wink. "Hey, sis. Be right with you." Then he turned his attention back to Macy again.

Laughing, Macy pushed his face back. "Stop. You're embarrassing Elizabeth. And why didn't you call and tell me you were coming home?" she scolded. "I could've had dinner ready."

Setting her on her feet again, he swept off his hat and ruffled his hair. "I wanted to surprise you."

"Well, I'm surprised, all right."

"And I'm leaving," Elizabeth interjected as she moved to the door. She paused on the stoop and looked back. "Now, don't you two do anything I wouldn't do," she lectured sternly, then fluttered her fingers in farewell and closed the door.

Macy turned back to Rory, then grinned and threw her arms around his neck. "I'm so glad you're home. I've been bored out of my mind."

Scooping her up into his arms again, he strode for her bunk. "Well, it just so happens I have a cure for boredom."

Smiling, she dragged a finger down the slope of his nose. "And what would that be?"

"Lose those clothes and I'll show you."

Macy sat cross-legged on the bed opposite Rory, a plate of cheese and crackers perched on a pillow between them.

"I swear the man's a genius," she said. "He's rigged up this water system where each plant is watered individually and he figured out a way to fertilize them, using the same system. The fertilizer he uses is drippings from his compost pile, which must be really great stuff, because his plants are super healthy and beautiful to boot.

"And his gardens," she continued, her eyes bright with excitement. "They're unbelievable, and he's done all the work himself."

Chuckling, Rory popped a chunk of cheese into his mouth. "Much more and you're going to make me think the man can walk on water."

"I wouldn't be surprised if he could," she said. "He's really shy and doesn't say much. And when he does talk, he doesn't waste any words."

"What did you say this guy's name was?"

"John Sullivan. Do you know him?"

Rory frowned a minute, then shook his head. "Doesn't ring a bell."

"It probably wouldn't. He told me he doesn't come into town very much. Only when he has to. I think he's sort of a recluse. When I first saw him out in front of your store, he was standing by one of the mountain laurels and had a knife in his hand."

"A knife?" Rory repeated in alarm.

"Not a big one," she said, as if the size mattered. "Just a pocketknife. I thought he was going to do something to one of the trees, so I ran over to stop him. That's when I—"

He jackknifed up, knocking the plate from the pillow and scattering chunks of cheese across the bed.

"Are you nuts? The guy could have sliced you to ribbons."

Giving him a pained look, she began to pick up the cheese. "It wasn't a big knife," she said again. "And he wasn't going to cut me to ribbons. He was just checking for bores on the tree."

"How do you know that's what he was doing with the knife?"

She leaned to set the plate on the floor. "Because I saw the bores," she said as she straightened. "Which really makes me mad. I bought those trees at Arnold's nursery and I'm almost sure they weren't infected when I bought them. I said as much to John, and he told me some things that makes me think Arnold isn't a reputable nurseryman, that he's more interested in the money he can make than the quality of the plants he sells.

"I mentioned to John that I was considering opening a nursery here, and he said that a good one is needed. I'm thinking that I might talk to John, feel him out to see if he'd be interested in working for me, if I should decide to open a nursery, because I think he'd be a real asset as an employee. He's obviously very good with plants, if his gardens are any indication. And he's—"

Rory held up a hand, unable to get beyond the fact that when Macy had first seen John, he'd had a knife in his hand. "Whoa. Slow down a minute. Don't go offering this guy a job. You don't know anything about him. He could be a real nutcase, for all you know."

"He's nothing of the sort," she said defensively.

"In fact, when I caught him trying to look at my breasts, I—"

Rory came up off the pillow, his hands doubled into fists. "He did *what?*"

She patted at the air between them. "Calm down. He wasn't really looking at my breasts. I just *thought* he was. He was admiring my locket."

Flopping back against the pillow, he folded his arms across his chest. "Sure he was," he said dryly.

"He was," she insisted. "And he was really embarrassed that I thought he was sneaking a peek."

"I don't want you going to his house anymore."

Her chest swelled in defiance. "I beg your pardon, but I'll go wherever I want."

Realizing that he'd approached this all wrong, he caught her hand and dragged her over to sit beside him. "I'm not trying to tell you what to do," he said patiently.

She turned her face away to glare at the wall. "Well, it certainly sounds like it."

He caught her chin and forced her face back to his. "I'm only concerned about you. You don't know anything about this guy."

"And you do?" she challenged.

"No, but I intend to." He looped an arm around her shoulders and pulled her to his side. "I have to go back to Houston tomorrow, but before I leave, we'll pay Maw Parker a visit. See what she knows. If Maw says this guy's all right, then I won't say another word, I promise." He tipped her face up to his. "I'm not trying to control you, Macy," he said softly. "I just want to make sure you're safe. Okay?"

She pouted a moment longer, then mumbled a grudging "Okay."

* * *

"Maw, this is Macy Keller," Rory said, making the introductions. "Macy, Maw Parker."

Maw gave Macy a quick look-over. "So you're the gal who's trying to find her daddy. Rory told me about you."

Macy smiled weakly. "Yes, ma'am. I'm the one."

"Had any luck?" Maw asked.

Macy shook her head. "No, ma'am. Not yet."

"Listen, Maw," Rory said, anxious to get to the point of their visit. "I'm a bit pressed for time, but I'm hoping that you can help me out by giving me some information."

Swelling her chest a bit, Maw gave her dress a tug over her hips. "You came to the right person. If Maw don't know, nobody does."

Chuckling, Rory nodded his head. "Yes, ma'am. That's why I'm here." Sobering, he tugged Macy closer to his side and looped an arm around her waist. "Macy met a man the other day. John Sullivan. Do you know him?"

Maw flapped a hand. "I know him, all right. Spook. That's what everybody around here calls him."

"Spook?" Rory repeated, not liking the sound of the nickname. "Why's he called that?"

"'Cause he's weird," Maw said bluntly.

Rory gave Macy an I-told-you-so smirk, then said to Maw, "I had a feeling he was. Macy said the first time she saw him he had a knife in his hand. Claimed he was checking a tree for bores."

"Probably was," Maw replied with a shrug. "Spook knows more about plants than anybody I know, and that's saying something. Spends all his time shut up in those greenhouses he keeps behind his house. Folks say he even talks to them.''

''I talk to plants,'' Macy interjected, then gave Rory a bland look. ''Does that make me weird, too?''

Scowling, he turned his attention back to Maw. ''Macy went out to his house to see his greenhouses and now she wants to go back. I don't think she should. The guy could be dangerous.''

Maw lifted a brow. ''Spook dangerous?'' She hooted a laugh. ''That man probably grieves over every bug he has to kill.'' She shook her head. ''Spook may be weird, but he's not dangerous.''

Macy dug her elbow into Rory's ribs. ''See?'' she said smugly. ''I told you he was all right.''

Nine

Macy couldn't wait to return to John's house. Once Rory left for Houston, she climbed into her Jeep and made the long, winding drive to his farm. Seeing Old Blue parked beside the house, she considered knocking on his front door, then remembered Maw saying that he spent all of his time in his greenhouses. Figuring that's where she'd find him, she strode around back and headed for the greenhouse she'd visited the previous day.

"John?" she called as she stepped inside. She heard a clatter of metal, as if something had been dropped, then John appeared at the end of the middle walkway.

Smiling, she lifted a hand in greeting and started toward him. "I didn't mean to startle you. I started to stop at the house, but I figured I'd find you out here."

He stooped and picked up the watering can he'd dropped, then slowly straightened and set it aside. "Here's where I usually am."

"I hope you don't mind that I dropped by. I really enjoyed seeing your greenhouse yesterday and would like to see the other one, if you don't mind."

He dropped his gaze, his fingers sliding up and down the watering can's handle. "Not much to see. Just plants."

"They may be *just plants* to some," she informed him. "But I recognize quality when I see it."

He dragged a hand uneasily down his thigh, then nodded and turned for a rear door. "The other house is where I keep my tropicals," he said as he led the way out. "Keep it a bit warmer. More humidity in the air."

Macy followed, immediately adjusting her mind to his economy words, even finding comfort in their natural rhythm and the huskiness of his voice.

She spent the next hour trailing along behind him, listening in fascination as he described the different plants and told her how he'd obtained his cuttings of the rarer species.

By the time they reached the end of the tour, Macy wasn't at all ready to leave.

"Could you use any help?" she asked, then blushed and ducked her head. "I know that's presumptuous of me to ask," she said, then looked at him, her eyes filled with hope. "But I really miss working around plants, and I've got nothing but time on my hands."

He shuffled his feet a moment, seeming reluctant, then gave his chin a jerk. "I suppose you could deadhead the plants in the front garden if you want. That's where I was headed next.''

Though deadheading plants was a boring job that required very little brains, Macy would have agreed to do almost anything that would keep her from sitting in her trailer all day.

Barely able to contain her excitement, she spread a hand. ''After you,'' she said, then followed him out.

Later that night, Macy lay propped up in her bed, the legal pad on her lap and the phone book open at her side. She scanned the pages looking for a listing for Willie Cyrus, the name of one of the men Rory had recognized in the picture. Not finding the name, she began her search again, looking for one that might be close. Spotting a listing for a W. L. Cyrus, she quickly jotted the number and accompanying address beneath Willie's name on her pad, then placed a question mark after it, as a reminder to herself to verify the man was in fact Willie before approaching him.

Her eyes burning from looking at the small print so long, with a sigh, she set the pad aside and stretched. A glance at her wristwatch drew a frown. It was after ten and she hadn't heard from Rory yet. She hesitated a moment, then picked up her cell phone and punched in his number. She was tired after working in John's garden all day and was ready to go to sleep.

Settling back against her pillow, she listened to four rings, then frowned when his recorded message clicked on. She waited for the click, then said, ''Hi, Rory. It's me. If you get this message tonight, don't call me back. I'm going to bed.'' She covered her mouth, stifling a yawn, then added wearily, "I'm really sleepy. I worked with John—Spook to you," she added wryly, "and I'm pooped. I'm going out to his house again tomorrow, but I'll have my cell phone with me, so call me when you have a chance. Later."

After punching the disconnect button, she placed her phone on top of the pad, then gathered the clutter into a pile and set it down on the floor beside her bed. Yawning again, she stretched to switch off the light, then curled up on her side and pulled the sheet to her chin.

A smile curved her lips as she imagined herself as she'd been that day, standing in the middle of John's garden, surrounded by the beauty of his flowers and breathing their perfumed scent. The only thing that would have made her day better was if Rory had been with her to enjoy it.

She missed him. He hadn't been gone a day, and she missed him. She had so much to tell him, so many things she wanted to share with him. She wanted to tell him about her day. Share with him her impressions of John. Discuss with him the possibility of her opening a business in Tanner's Crossing. She wanted to stay here with him. Be near him. She prayed that's what he wanted, too.

"Tomorrow," she promised herself, and closed her eyes. She'd talk to him tomorrow when he returned from Houston.

Rory popped the last bite of his hamburger into his mouth, then shut off his truck's engine and opened his door. Eating on the run wasn't something he usually did, but things had been so crazy at the store that day, it was either grab a burger and fries from a fast-food joint on the way back to his apartment or starve. Starving held little appeal.

With a glance at his wristwatch, he loped up the steps that led to his apartment, anxious to get inside and call Macy before it got any later. He felt badly that he hadn't already called her, but he simply hadn't had the time.

No, he corrected. He could have called her while he was driving to his apartment. But he'd wanted to be piled up in his bed with her when he talked to her, not driving his truck. He wanted to hear her voice coming from the pillow next to his. Needed to hear it. He chuckled as he dug a hand into his pocket for his keys. What he really wanted, was *her* in his bed. Not just her voice.

He stuck the key in the lock, then stilled, realizing for the first time how strongly he felt about Macy. Stronger than he'd ever felt about anyone. He waited for the panic to hit, the urge to run as hard and fast as he could in the opposite direction. But he felt nothing. Not panic, anyway. The only urge he had was to talk to Macy. To hear her voice.

"Hi, Rory."

Startled, he glanced over and bit back a groan when he saw Andrea, a neighbor with whom he'd shared a brief and regrettable affair, walking his way. He wasn't thrilled to see her. To be honest, he'd thought she'd given up the chase months ago.

He twisted open the door and stuffed his keys back into his pocket, hoping to get rid of her quickly. "Hey, Andrea. How's it going?"

"Not very well. It seems I've locked myself out of

my apartment.'' She pushed her lips out into a little-girl pout and dragged a finger down his arm. ''I was hoping you'd let me crash at your place.''

It was a lie and Rory knew it. It was a ruse to get into his bed.

And he only wanted one woman in his bed. Macy.

''Call a locksmith,'' he suggested, and stepped inside his apartment and out of her reach.

''I can't. My cell phone is in my apartment.''

Stifling a sigh, he dragged open the door. ''You can use mine, but make it quick. I want to get a shower.''

Looking pleased with herself, she breezed inside and closed the door behind her.

He gestured toward the phone on the end table as he toed off his boots. ''There's the phone.''

Instead of crossing to the end table, she headed for him. Caught with a boot half on and half off, Rory was a sitting duck.

She slipped her arms around his neck. ''I know where the phone is.'' She pressed her breasts against his chest and added in a sultry voice, ''The same as I know where your bed is.''

Scowling, he kicked off the boot and reached to drag her arms from around his neck. ''No way, Andrea. I told you. It's over.'' He gestured at the phone again. ''You said you wanted to make a call.''

With a huff, she stalked to the phone and picked it up. She placed it to her ear, then held it out to him. ''It's dead.''

Swearing, he snatched his cell phone from the clip on his belt, tossed it to her, then turned for his bedroom. "Lock the door behind you when you leave," he called over his shoulder.

To make certain she didn't attempt to join him in the shower, he slammed the bathroom door behind him, then twisted the lock.

Ten minutes later, he stepped out of the bathroom, a towel wrapped around his waist, and took a quick glance around. Relieved to find Andrea was gone, he blew out a breath and headed for the kitchen. He pulled a beer from the refrigerator, popped the top, then crossed back into the den to retrieve his cell. Frowning, he looked around, wondering where Andrea had put it. It wasn't on the coffee table or the end table. He flipped up the sofa cushions, thinking maybe it had slipped between the cushions. Not finding it there, he spun angrily for his bedroom. "The bitch," he muttered darkly. She was using the phone as a ploy to get him into her apartment. Well, she could have the damn phone, he thought as he ripped off his towel. He wasn't going anywhere near her.

Groaning, he dropped down on the side of the bed. But without a phone, he couldn't call Macy. He started to rise, planning to dress and go in search of a pay phone so that he could call her, then sagged back down again. Hell, he couldn't call her. He didn't know her damn number! He had it saved on his cell phone, but that wasn't going to do him a damn bit of good now.

Sighing, he fell back across his bed. He'd call one of his brothers in the morning. Have one of them get a message to Macy to let her know he wouldn't be home for at least another day. It was a hell of a way to communicate with the woman you'd just realized you'd fallen in love with, but it was the best he could do at the moment.

As Macy sipped her morning cup of coffee, she flipped aimlessly through the stack of photos lying on the table. It wasn't that she found the pictures particularly interesting. She just didn't have anything else to do. With no TV, no radio and no Rory around to entertain her, the photos were her only escape from total boredom.

Selecting one from the pile, she sank back, sipping her coffee as she studied the people pictured. She had to agree with Elizabeth, she thought, wrinkling her nose in distaste at the ladies' fashions. She'd never be caught dead wearing a skirt that short, either.

But Darla Jean certainly hadn't seemed to have a problem with her skirt's length. In fact, judging by the way she had her legs crossed, showing off a shamefully long length of leg, she appeared to enjoy the style.

With a sigh, she leaned to toss the picture back onto the table and snagged another before settling back and taking another sip of her coffee. She bit back a smile when she spotted the man Elizabeth had said reminded her of Whit. He did have Whit's mannerisms, she thought. He stood on the fringes, his hands stuffed into his pockets, as if reluctant to join the group. Though everyone else was smiling at the camera, he was looking away, frowning slightly, as if he didn't like having his picture taken.

She glanced at the time again, then dropped the photo onto the pile and stood, draining the last of her coffee in one greedy gulp. She'd told John she'd ar-

rive early that day, so that she could help him trans-
plant some antique roses that needed moving, and she
didn't want to be late.

Knowing John, he probably wouldn't wait on her,
and she didn't want to miss out on all the fun.

Macy braced her shovel against the ground and
dragged a weary hand across her brow. They'd been
at it a good two hours and she was in need of a break.
Thinking a drink of water would go down good about
now, she turned to ask John's permission to go inside
his house. But the request lodged in her throat as a
sense of déjà vu swept over her. He stood in profile
to her, frowning at something off in the distance, his
cap pushed back far on his head and his hands shoved
deeply into his pockets. She strained, trying to think
what it was that was so familiar about the scene, why
she felt such a strong sense that she'd experienced it
before.

The blood drained from her face as she realized the
reason. The pictures she had looked at that morning.
The man who had stood on the fringes, his face turned
away. The man had looked like Whit, she remembered thinking. A part of the group, yet separate from
them. Different. Aloof.

Her heart pounding, she glanced around, taking in
her surroundings. The cottage-style garden that surrounded his house. The greenhouses behind it. His
love of plants that mirrored so closely her own.

No, she told herself, and gulped back the panic that
squeezed at her throat. John Sullivan wasn't her father. It wasn't possible. Her mother would never have

been interested in a man like John. He was plain, uninspiring. Poor.

But then she remembered catching him staring at her necklace. The expression on his face. She closed her fingers around the locket, its miniature hinges cutting against her skin as she clutched it tightly in her palm. It wasn't possible, she told herself, and made herself look his way again. Tears welled in her eyes as she stared at him, unable to bring herself to ask him the question that burned in her soul.

"John?"

He glanced her way and she stared into eyes the same shade of amber as her own.

She gulped, swallowed. "Did you know a woman named Darla Jean Keller?"

He didn't move so much as a muscle for what seemed like an eternity. When he did move, it was to look away.

He dragged his cap low over his forehead and picked up his shovel. "Maybe."

Her heart seemed to stop, then wedge itself in her throat. "She was my mother," she whispered, her voice trembling.

He thrust the shovel into the soil surrounding a rosebush. "Figured she was."

She waited for him to say more. When he didn't, she dropped her own shovel and crossed to him, her legs wooden, each stride that brought her closer to him seemed a mile long. "Are you my father?"

He lifted the shovelful of dirt and dumped it into the pile he'd made. "No."

Frustration boiled up inside her. "Look at me!"

she cried. "Look at me and tell me that you're not my father."

He braced the shovel against the ground, then slowly turned to meet her gaze, his eyes flat, emotionless. "I'm not your father."

He was lying. She knew he was. Anger and grief welled inside her, each fighting for dominance of her emotions. She wouldn't cry, she told herself. She wouldn't let him see her tears. But they were there, burning behind her eyes.

She grabbed the locket and ripped it off, snapping the thin chain in two. With her gaze on his, she threw it down at his feet, then wheeled and ran for her Jeep.

She made it as far as the main highway before she was forced to pull over, blinded by tears. Folding her arms over the steering wheel, she dropped her head on them and gave in to the tears. She wept until there were no more tears left to weep, until only a gaping hole remained in her heart.

Rory.

She needed him. Needed to feel the comfort of his arms around her. His strength.

She groped blindly for her cell phone and punched his number. She sniffed and dragged a hand beneath her nose while she waited through two rings.

"Hello?"

Startled by the feminine voice that answered, for a moment she couldn't speak.

"Hello?" the voice said again.

"I'm sorry," Macy said quickly, then sniffed again. "I must have dialed the wrong number." She started to draw the phone from her ear, but stopped when she heard the woman say, "Were you calling for Rory?"

She slowly drew the phone back to her ear. "Yes."

"I'm sorry," the woman said. "But he's...indisposed at the moment. Can I give him a message?"

Macy shook her head, then made herself say. "N-no, thank you."

She dropped the phone to her lap and stared out the windshield, trying to think of a logical explanation for a woman answering Rory's phone. She was an employee, she told herself. Someone who worked at his store.

But the woman's sleepy voice, her smugness when she'd finally offered the word *indisposed* to explain why Rory couldn't come to the phone ruled out that possibility and made Macy face the ugly truth.

Rory might be the only man in her life, but she wasn't the only woman in his.

Living in a trailer made it easy to put a town behind you. Macy accomplished the task in less than thirty minutes, after returning from John's. She latched down the cabinets and doors inside, unhooked the trailer from the electrical and plumbing connections, then hitched it to the rear of her Jeep and pulled out of the park that had been her home for the last month.

There was no one to say goodbye to, no one to wish her well on her journey. She left Tanner's Crossing the same way in which she'd arrived.

Alone.

Rory made the turn into the trailer park, then jerked his foot off the accelerator and did a double-take, sure that he wasn't seeing what he thought he was seeing. But when he looked the second time, Macy's trailer was still gone.

Stunned, he pulled to a stop in front of the empty space where the trailer had been and stared. She was gone, he told himself. But where? Thinking Woodrow would know, since it was Woodrow he'd asked to deliver his message to her, he reached for his cell phone then swore when he remembered Andrea had it. Hopping down from his truck, he strode across the street and knocked on the door of the trailer parked there. The door opened a crack and a woman's face appeared in the narrow opening.

"Yes?" she asked suspiciously.

"Could I borrow your phone, please?" Rory asked. "I need to make a call."

She glanced over his head at his truck, then shifted her gaze back to his. "If you're looking for that woman whose trailer was parked over there, she's gone."

Rory bit down on his impatience. "Yes, ma'am. I can see that she is. But I need to call my brother and find out if he knows where she went."

"Is your brother a big man?"

"Yes."

"I doubt he knows. He was here a couple of hours ago looking for her, too. I told him the same as you. She's already gone."

Dragging a hand over his hair in frustration, Rory turned away. "Thanks," he muttered.

Once behind the wheel of his truck again, Rory headed for Maw Parker's store. Not that he expected

Maw to know where Macy was. But Maw did know where John Sullivan lived, and he figured if anyone knew Macy's whereabouts, Spook would be the one who'd know.

Rory pulled up behind the old blue truck, then jumped down. "Sullivan?" he called as he swung open the garden gate that led to the house. "Sullivan!" he shouted impatiently.

When he didn't hear a reply, he stopped and looked around. Seeing freshly turned dirt near the low fence, he walked over to take a closer look. A shovel lay on the ground near the pile, and Rory, out of habit, stooped to pick it up. As he did, he saw a glimmer of metal in the dirt. Dread filled him and he tossed aside the shovel and dropped to his knees to smooth the dirt away. "Oh, God, no," he moaned as he drew the broken chain and locket from the dirt.

"What are you doin' here? This is private property."

Rory spun to his feet, the necklace clenched in his fist. Anger boiled inside him as he met John Sullivan's gaze. "Where is she?" he growled. "What have you done with Macy?"

"She left. Hours ago."

Rory stalked toward him. "You're lyin'. Macy's gone. Her trailer's gone. What have you done to her?"

"Nothin'. I told you. She left. I never laid a hand on her."

If the man was afraid of Rory, he gave no sign of his fear. He stood straight as a board and waited. Rory threw a punch that sent Spook staggering back two steps. While he was off balance, Rory dove into his chest, knocking him flat on his back. With Spook pinned beneath him, Rory closed a hand over the man's throat and lifted his fist that held the necklace. "Then tell me why I found this lying in the dirt."

"She left it there," Spook choked out.

"She wouldn't have left it there on purpose," Rory shouted. "She always wore it. She never took it off."

Spook closed his hands around the one Rory held at his neck and pulled, trying to break his hold. "Swear she did…mad…wouldn't admit to bein' her father."

Rory froze at the word *father*. "You're Macy's father?"

His face red, his eyes bulging, Spook nodded.

Rory slowly loosened his grip. "You're Macy's father," he repeated dully, trying to absorb the fact.

Gasping, Spook tried to sit up. "Yes."

Rory pushed off the man and to his feet. "You hurt her," he said, then clenched his hand more tightly around the necklace. "By refusing to claim her, you broke her heart. Dammit!" he swore and turned away. "She needs me. I know she does. And I don't have a clue where she is."

"I didn't mean to hurt her," Spook said from behind him.

Rory swung around to glare at him. "Well, that's exactly what you did. She wanted so badly to find her father. And when she finally did, you shunned her, just like you did her mother."

Spook shook his head. "I never shunned Darla Jean. I loved her. She was the one who shunned me. Left here and never came back."

"Did you know she was pregnant when she left?" Rory demanded.

Setting his jaw, Spook looked away. "I knew," he said after a minute. "But knowing didn't do me no good. Darla Jean didn't want me for a husband and she sure as hell didn't want me claiming our child."

The anger sagged from Rory at the misery in the man's voice.

"I've got to find her," he said and turned for his truck.

"Wait."

Rory turned.

"When you do," Spook said, then gestured at the necklace Rory held in his fist. "Give that back to her. Tell her I want her to keep it. It was her mother's. I know, 'cause I was the one who gave it to Darla Jean."

There were times in his life when Rory had wished he wasn't a Tanner. But at the moment, he was glad for the power associated with the name. The name Tanner pulled strings and got favors that other folks would never receive.

After explaining his situation to the sheriff, the sheriff not only promised Rory that he'd put out an all-points bulletin for Macy's Jeep and trailer, but he also loaned Rory a cell phone, so that the sheriff could call him once the Jeep was spotted.

It hadn't taken long for the call to come in. Macy's Jeep was spotted in a trailer park off of Highway 290, just south of Austin. With his path cleared for him by the highway patrol, Rory raced his way through towns and along highways, cutting the normal driving time to reach her location by at least half.

By the time he pulled his truck in behind her Jeep, darkness had settled over the landscape. With a tip of his hat to the highway patrolman who had led the way, Rory jogged for the trailer door.

He pounded a fist against it and yelled, "Macy! Open up. It's me. Rory."

He listened, waiting for her response. When he didn't hear one, he pounded again. Harder. "Macy!" he yelled. "Either you open up this door or I'm beating it down. The choice is yours."

The door pushed open, striking Rory on the head and knocking off his hat. Dazed by the blow, he swayed drunkenly on his feet.

"What do you want?"

He blinked her into focus, then set his jaw and grabbed hold of the door. "You," he said angrily, and pushed her back.

Once inside, he turned on her. "What the hell do you think you were doing by leaving town, without telling me where you were going?"

She folded her arms across her chest. "You aren't my guardian. I'm a grown woman and can come and go as I please."

"Well, I may not be your guardian, but I think I have a right to know your plans. For God's sake, Macy!" he cried. "Do you realize how scared I was when I found your trailer gone? The trouble I had to go to to finally track you down?" He tossed up his hands. "Hell, I could be in prison for murder right now, and it would be your damn fault if I was."

"Mine!" she cried. "I didn't do anything to you."

"You sure as hell didn't," he shot back. "You didn't even give me the courtesy of a call."

"I *did* call you! If you don't believe me, just ask your girlfriend."

"You damn sure—" Rory stopped, then dropped his face to his hands with a groan. "Andrea," he muttered. He inhaled a deep breath, then lifted his head. "Macy, I didn't have my phone. Andrea took it."

She shot a hand beneath her nose. "It isn't my fault you loan your phone to your girlfriends."

"Andrea's not my girlfriend. She's a neighbor in Houston. She was locked out of her apartment and stopped by to borrow my phone. The land line was dead, so I gave her my cell."

"That was awfully generous of you. Cell phones don't come cheap."

Frustrated, Rory drew in a deep breath. "I didn't *give* her the phone. I loaned it to her. She left while I was in the shower and took it with her."

"Shower?" she repeated, then clapped her hands over her ears. "No. I don't want to hear any more. Just leave."

He took a step toward her. "I'm not leaving, Macy. Not without you. I talked to Spook."

She bent double, her arms hugged around her middle, as if he'd punched her in the stomach.

He dropped down on a knee in front of her and reached to lay a hand on her cheek. "He told me he was your father." He reached into his pocket and pulled out the necklace. "He asked me to give you this. Told me to tell you that he had given it to your mother and that he wanted you to keep it."

Her face crumpled at the sight of the necklace, and she sank to her knees and covered her face with her hands. Rory wrapped his arms around her. "I think you need to give him a chance, Macy," he said softly. "It wasn't his decision not to claim you. It was your mother's."

"He lied," she cried and sobbed harder. "He told me he wasn't my father."

He tightened his arms around her and laid his head against hers. "I know how much that must have hurt. This isn't going to be easy. For either of you. It was a shock for him to see you. He made the connection long before you did. And it hurt. Opened up old wounds that I'm sure he thought had healed long ago."

She buried her face in the curve of his neck. "I don't know what to do. What to say."

"You don't have to say or do anything right now," he assured her. "Give yourself some time. You both need that." He drew back and tipped her face up to his. "And when you're ready to talk to him, you won't be alone. I'll be with you."

Fresh tears welled in her eyes. "You?"

He nodded. "You're not ever going to have to face anything alone again. I'm going to be right by your side. I love you, Macy. I should have told you that before now. But the fact that I didn't doesn't change how I feel."

She drew her hands to her lips, her fingers trembling. "Oh, Rory," she whispered. "I didn't think you did. I thought I was just another woman in your life."

He heaved a weary sigh. "You know, I worked

damn hard to earn my reputation, but it looks like I'm going to have to work a lot harder to live it down.''

When she merely stared at him, he shook his head. ''Just know this,'' he said and reached to thread a lock of hair behind her ear, ''from this day forward, you're the *only* woman in my life.'' He drew his hand to her cheek and looked her square in the eye. ''Understand?''

Tears brimmed in her eyes and she nodded. ''I do.''

He gathered his hands in hers and squeezed. ''I'd like to hear you say those two words again sometime soon. Say, about a week?''

Her eyes rounded. ''Are you asking me to marry you?''

''Well, yeah,'' he said, then laughed. ''You didn't think I expected you to live in sin with me, did you?''

''I just wanted to be sure.''

He stood and drew her to her feet, then sank down on a knee, holding her hands between his. ''Macy Keller, would you do me the honor of taking my name and becoming my wife?''

She bit her lip to stem the tears. ''Oh, Rory. All my life, I wanted to be a Tanner.'' She sank to her knees in front of him. ''But to be given the name by you is better. So much better.''

Epilogue

When they reached the front door of the farmhouse, Rory gave Macy's hand a squeeze. "Sure you don't want me to go in with you?" he asked in concern.

Though tempted to accept his offer of support, Macy shook her head. "No. I need to do this alone."

Nodding his head in understanding, he gave her hand another squeeze, then released it. "I'll be in the truck, if you need me. Take as long as you want."

"Thanks, Rory."

She watched until he reached his truck, then took a deep breath and turned to knock on the door. It opened almost immediately and she found herself looking up into eyes almost the exact shade of amber as her own. She stared in silence, unsure what to say, what to do.

Without a word, John stepped back, allowing her

room to enter. Her knees a little unsteady, she stepped into the small living room and stopped to look around. The furnishings in the room were as simple and un-assuming as the man who had selected them, yet she felt the warmth of each worn piece, its comfort, en-velop her. This was her father's house, yet this was the first time she had ever seen it.

Tears welled in her eyes and she turned to John and lifted her hands helplessly. "I don't know what to say to you."

He dropped his chin to his chest. "Not much to be said," he said, then shook his head and frowned, as if knowing what a ridiculous statement that was to make. Years stood between them. Years in which they should have been building memories, a relationship. Yet, here they stood, virtual strangers.

"It wasn't that I didn't want you," he began slowly. "Darla Jean…she didn't want me."

"But she became pregnant with your child," Macy reminded him stubbornly. "Surely you must have had some kind of relationship with her."

Turning away, he stuffed his hands in his pockets and stared out the front window. "We did, of sorts. But I was nothin' but a dirt-poor farmer. Not the kind of man she wanted to be seen with or settle down with. She had a hankerin' for fine things. Things she knew I'd never be able to give her. I loved Darla Jean with all my heart, but she never loved me."

Macy heard the pain in his voice, the shame. But it was the regret that melted every ounce of resent-ment she harbored toward him for all the lost years. She wasn't the only one Darla Jean had hurt. John had suffered, too.

She slipped her hand into her pocket and fingered the locket. "I think she did," she said quietly.

He glanced over his shoulder to look at her.

Closing her fingers around the locket, she took a step toward him. "After Mother died, it was my job to dispose of all her possessions. I kept very few of her personal things, as we had totally different tastes. But there was one piece of her jewelry that I kept." She drew her hand from her pocket and held up the necklace, the locket dangling from its end. "This."

She watched his gaze slide to the locket, the slow bob of his Adam's apple as he stared, and knew now what she needed to say to John, what she needed to do.

"She loved you," she whispered. "She never wore the locket, but she kept it all these years. That tells me that she cared about it, as well as the man who gave it to her."

John lifted his head to look at her, and her tears welled higher at the hope that filled his eyes. Taking his hand, she placed the necklace on his palm and closed his fingers around it. "Keep it as a memory of Darla Jean. I think that would please her."

He opened his hand to stare at the locket. A fat tear rolled down his face and dropped onto the tarnished gold heart. Gulping, he shook his head. "Rory said that I hurt you when I refused to admit that I was your father." He lifted his head to meet Macy's gaze. "I didn't mean to hurt you. Figured you'd be ashamed if you learned the truth. Figured you wouldn't want folks around town knowing I was the one who fathered you."

Choked by the emotion that filled her throat, Macy

shook her head. "No, I'm not ashamed. I'd be proud for everyone to know that you're my father." She took a deep breath, desperately wanting to touch him, hold him as much as she needed to be held. "If it's all right, I'd like to hug you."

He blanched, obviously terrified at the thought then gulped and slowly nodded. Cautiously Macy stepped closer and wrapped her arms around him. He stood stiff as a poker through three heartbeats, then slowly lifted his arms and draped them around her. She felt the tremble of his body, the hesitancy. But she felt the yearning, too, and knew that even though they had a long way to go in developing a relationship, she had finally found the father she had so desperately wanted.

"Is everything okay in here?"

At the sound of Rory's voice, Macy glanced over her shoulder to find Rory peering around the front door, his face creased with worry. Smiling, she stepped from John's arms and held out her hand to him. "Everything's fine," she assured him.

With a sigh of relief, he stepped inside and took her hand. "Well?" he said, looking back and forth between the two. "How have y'all decided to handle this?"

Macy looked hopefully at John. "I'm not sure that we have. But if John's willing, I think I've found the man I want to give me away at our wedding."

The blood drained from John's face. "Give you away?" he repeated hoarsely.

Rory slung an arm around Macy's shoulders. "Yep. Macy and I are getting married. He gave John a slow perusal. "And I have a western suit in my store that I think will be perfect for the father of the bride.''

John's knees buckled and he sat down hard on the sofa. "Father of the bride," he repeated dully, staring up at the two. He puffed his cheeks and blew out a long breath. "Imagine that. Me, father of the bride."

"Better get used to the sound of it pretty darn quick," Rory warned him. He looked down at Macy and shot her a wink. "'Cause we plan to stick you with another title pretty soon. That of grandfather."

Macy gaped. "I'm not pregnant!" she cried.

His smile smug, Rory hugged her up against his side and turned for the door. "Maybe not now. But you will be before long, if I have anything to say about it."

* * * * *

presents

You're on his hit list.

Enjoy the next title in

Katherine Garbera's
King of Hearts miniseries:

MISTRESS MINDED
(Silhouette Desire #1587)

When a workaholic boss persuades his faithful
assistant to pretend to be his temporary
mistress, it's going to take the influence of
a matchmaking angel-in-training to bring
them together permanently!

*Available June 2004
at your favorite retail outlet.*

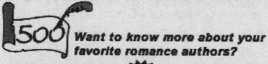

If you enjoyed what you just read,
then we've got an offer you can't resist!

Take 2 bestselling
love stories FREE!
Plus get a FREE surprise gift!

Clip this page and mail it to Silhouette Reader Service™

IN U.S.A.	**IN CANADA**
3010 Walden Ave.	P.O. Box 609
P.O. Box 1867	Fort Erie, Ontario
Buffalo, N.Y. 14240-1867	L2A 5X3

YES! Please send me 2 free Silhouette Desire® novels and my free surprise gift. After receiving them, if I don't wish to receive anymore, I can return the shipping statement marked cancel. If I don't cancel, I will receive 6 brand-new novels every month, before they're available in stores! In the U.S.A., bill me at the bargain price of $3.57 plus 25¢ shipping and handling per book and applicable sales tax, if any*. In Canada, bill me at the bargain price of $4.24 plus 25¢ shipping and handling per book and applicable taxes**. That's the complete price and a savings of at least 10% off the cover prices—what a great deal! I understand that accepting the 2 free books and gift places me under no obligation ever to buy any books. I can always return a shipment and cancel at any time. Even if I never buy another book from Silhouette, the 2 free books and gift are mine to keep forever.

225 SDN DNUP
326 SDN DNUQ

Name	(PLEASE PRINT)	
Address	Apt.#	
City	State/Prov.	Zip/Postal Code

* Terms and prices subject to change without notice. Sales tax applicable in N.Y.
** Canadian residents will be charged applicable provincial taxes and GST.
  All orders subject to approval. Offer limited to one per household and not valid to current Silhouette Desire® subscribers.
  ® are registered trademarks of Harlequin Books S.A., used under license.

DES02   ©1998 Harlequin Enterprises Limited

Award-winning author

Jennifer Greene

**invites readers to indulge in
the next compelling installment of**

The Scent of Lavender

The Campbell sisters awaken to passion
when love blooms where they least expect it!

WILD IN THE MOONLIGHT
(Silhouette Desire #1588)

When sexy Cameron Lachlan walked onto
Violet Campbell's lavender farm, he seduced
the cautious beauty in the blink of an eye.
Their passion burned hot and fast, but
could they form a relationship beyond
the bedroom door?

*Available June 2004
at your favorite retail outlet.*

COMING NEXT MONTH

#1585 CHALLENGED BY THE SHEIKH—Kristi Gold
Dynasties: The Danforths
Hotshot workaholic Imogene Danforth was up for a promotion, and only
her inability to ride a horse was standing in her way. Sheikh Raf Shakir
had vowed to train her on one of his prized Arabians…provided she stay
at his ranch. But what was Raf truly training Imogene to be: a wonderful
rider or his new bed partner?

#1586 THE BRIDE TAMER—Ann Major
Forced to rely on her wealthy in-laws, Vivian Escobar never dreamed
she'd meet a man as devastatingly sexy as Cash McRay—a man who was
set to marry her sister-in-law but who only had eyes for Vivian. Dare they
act on the passion between them? For their secret affair might very well
destroy a family.…

#1587 MISTRESS MINDED—Katherine Garbera
King of Hearts
With a lucrative contract on the line, powerful executive Adam Powell
offered his sweet assistant the deal of a lifetime—pretend to be his
mistress until the deal was sealed. Jayne Montrose was no fool; she knew
this was the perfect opportunity to finally get into Adam's bed…and into
his heart!

#1588 WILD IN THE MOONLIGHT—Jennifer Greene
The Scent of Lavender
She had a gift for making things grow…except when it came to
relationships. Then Cameron Lachlan walked onto Violet Campbell's
lavender farm and seduced her in the blink of an eye. Their passion
burned hot and fast, but could their blossoming romance overcome the
secret Violet kept?

#1589 HOLD ME TIGHT—Cait London
Heartbreakers
Desperate to hire the protective skills of Alexi Stepanov, Jessica Sterling
found herself offering him anything he wanted. She never imagined his
price would be so high, or that she would be so willing to give him
everything he demanded…and more.

#1590 HOT CONTACT—Susan Crosby
Behind Closed Doors
On forced leave from the job that was essentially his entire life, Detective
Joe Vicente was intrigued by P.I. Arianna Alvarado's request for his help.
He agreed to aid in her investigation, vowing not to become personally
involved. But Joe soon realized that Arianna was a temptation he might
not be able to resist.

SDCNM0504